High Plains Ambush

John D. Fie. Jr

Copyright © 2017 by Dusty Saddle Publishing

Formerly released as "Blood on the Plains"

ISBN: 9781521503591

All rights reserved. No part of this publication may be reproduced, distributed, or transmitted in any form or by any means, including photocopying, recording, or other electronic or mechanical methods, without the prior written permission of the publisher, except in the case of brief quotations embodied in critical reviews and certain other noncommercial uses permitted by copyright law.

ACKNOWLEDGMENT

I'd like to take the time to thank all my family and friends, and give a special thanks to all my readers who have helped make this book possible.

To all those at the State and National Parks, who were helpful in naming all the various different types of vegetation and wildlife that inhabited the different areas in which I visited to help create the storyline.

PORTRAIT OF A WRITING STAR

John D. Fie is the name to know in westerns. This rugged cowboy spent years on the road learning his trade and writing down stories. His kind of Americana can't be found many places anymore except on the pages of his novels.

Before I met John, I didn't have a true appreciation of what it meant to be a western writer. It wasn't long before his enthusiasm for the people, events, and places he memorializes began to be important to me. But that's the kind of man the author is and the kind of excitement you get from reading his stories.

The most difficult thing about reading a John D. Fie western is putting it down. I suggest, as a reader, you avoid the trouble and read them coast to coast. If you're like me, you'll be itching to get your hands on the next one.

Get ready for a ride on an unbroken horse down a rocky steep trail. This is the kind of book that makes you satisfied to be a reader. Come enjoy the story with me.

Bruce G. Bennett ~ Bestselling author of "Western Dawn."

Chapter One

Matt sat on the Mesa with his horse, Ole Friend for a long time, overlooking the valley floor and the town in the distance. There was a time when the Sioux nation hunted Buffalo here and held many ceremonies. This was known to them as Katie IMO (Enchanted Mesa). It was now full of farms and ranches and a growing town called Buffalo Flats.

Always talking to the roan made great company for Matt as he began telling the tale of the Great Sioux Nation. Of course, Ole Friend knew it well from hearing it so many times before.

"Our way of life is leaving us, Friend, going the way of the buffalo and the Sioux. Just look at all that, will you?" Matt Nodding his head towards, the settlement. "Settlers, city slickers, dudes and who knows what all?"

After all the year's Friend had been with Matt, the roan knew only too well how it was.

Buffalo as far as the eye could see, the Sioux on the hunt and the ceremonies after the hunt was now only a memory, a sad memory!

The Sioux was a big part of Matt's life after being found in a burning wagon as the only survivor of a massacre by the Blackfoot, the arch enemy of the Sioux.

'Ole Friend, the roan Matt was riding was a gift given to him by the great Sioux War Chief Buffalo Robe. A great honor that was bestowed on Matt for the counting of many coups in different wars with the Black Foot.

The Indian nations knew about Matt and the Roan by the distinct markings. Of the hand prints and stripes, on the roan's shoulders and flanks and the Roan seemed to know he was special, he was high spirited and carried Matt with pride.

Yes, there was no mistaking who was riding that Roan known to the Indian as Pahaska, the white man with long hair, Matt Hutchins.

"We best be getting on down there Friend, it's been a long time since I slept in a real feather bed and you a stall with hay and a bucket of oats."

So, with a soft coaching of the knees, Friend moved out and down the mesa toward the town of Buffalo Flats. Passing a few of the small farms on the way in, Matt couldn't help but notice the poor upkeep of the houses and farm buildings. He thought to himself, what did they expect in Buffalo country, evidently not real rich soil for crops?

As he entered the east end of town, all eyes were on the roan and the man riding him. It was a sight to see. Stopping in front of the livery stable, Matt was greeted by the stable hand.

"My horse needs a nice dry stall," Matt told the man. "Oats and a good rubdown."

The livery hand stood there and looked, saying, "Never seen nothing like you afore. Mountain Man are you?"

Matt ignored the man, flips him a couple of silver dollars for Friends care and asks, "Where's the best hotel in town?

Matt knew he had made a mistake as soon as he asked the question, because the man quickly asked, "Staying awhile are you?"

Matt knew that wherever he goes, it's always the same questions. He gives them no answers.

He looks up the street and spots a hotel. "That hotel up the block serve meals?"

The stable man was quick to respond. "Yes sir, they sure do, friend."

Giving the man a serious look, Matt says, "You give my horse the best care, he deserves it."

Matt turned and started walking toward the hotel.

The man thought better of his next question as he watched Matt leave and left it alone. He felt this Mountain Man was no one to fool with. After caring for the horse, the man heads to the Sheriff's office. The sheriff had left orders to be notified of any strangers in town. "Sheriff! Sheriff!" he said winded as he rushed into the office.

"We got us a stranger in town, and he's a real strange looking one at that."

Sheriff Fry, sitting behind his desk was trying to get some paperwork done, looks up at the livery stable hand.

"What's so strange about him Clem?" He laid the papers aside.

"Buckskins and the biggest Sharps rifle you ever did see, and he had twin 45's strapped to his hips. With Longhair with an Indian headband. He doesn't answer a question, just gives out orders and real mean like too."

The sheriff's interest now peeks, and he decides he better go and check this fellow out.

"Where is he, Clem?" Getting up from his desk, he straps his gun belt around his waist, reaches for his hat and puts it on.

Looking for the hotel, Clem gives the sheriff the thumb, "That way Sheriff, the hotel."

Not knowing what he might find, the sheriff decides to also carry the sawed-off shotgun, "Always best to be prepared Clem," he told the livery stable hand.

"Sheriff," Clem asked excitedly, "You think you'll need me to tag along?"

With a shake of his head the sheriff says, "Not this trip Clem, I don't believe that they'll be any problems." He knows having Clem along would only cause him to not only watch out for himself, but he'd have to worry about Clem.

Checking the chambers of the shotgun for load, he clicked the barrel shut and starts toward the hotel.

Storekeepers and passer-byes on the street know very well where the sheriff is heading. Word got around fast in this small settlement of Buffalo Flats.

It was a quiet little place where nothing ever seemed to happen since the new sheriff had been hired.

It appears the old sheriff left town for some strange reason. Word around town was he was chased out by the town council, and only they knew the reason why.

But peace now prevails with Sheriff Fry in town. He wasn't one to be played with, and that message got around real fast, to the surrounding counties that troublemakers weren't welcome in Buffalo Flats.

When the Cowboys from the ranches got their pay, they knew not to come to town and get drunk and loud.

Sheriff Fry always kept the cells full on pay days, and the big ranchers tried keeping as many ranch hands out of the city and piecemeal them on different days.

As the sheriff reached the doors of the hotel, thoughts of how to approach the stranger were on his mind. But hearing the conversation, he decides to hang back until he found out what it was all about. Keeping out of sight and listening, he heard the desk clerk telling the stranger no, about a room.

Matt tried, hungry and needing a bath was in no mood for the word no and began to demand a room.

Hearing enough and finding the stranger's reason for being here, the sheriff stepped into the room and says, "Alright, what's going on here? The two of you can be heard yelling halfway down the street."

The desk clerk, seeing the sheriff begins whining about this stranger, "He can't have the room."

"Why?" Was the sheriff's question to the clerk, who could only come up with the fact the stranger was dirty and smelled like buffalo.

Matt said a little too loudly, "Not Buffalo. Bear fat." He turned to the sheriff. "Sheriff, nobody likes being called, low count and high smelling."

With Matt's reply, the sheriff could only break out in a soft laugh, realizing the stranger wasn't the trouble. It was the clerk, and he was relieved the stranger wasn't the problem.

"Just give the man the room," Sheriff Fry ordered. "And stop judging people by their looks. This fella won't smell like buffalo or bear fat after a long hot bath."

He turned to Matt, "I got to be honest with you, Mister. I caught a good sniff myself when I came through the door. It's my delicate sense abilities that got offended."

"Well now, if that don't beat all," the clerk fussed. You're not gonna take his side on this, are you Sheriff? After all, this is my hotel, ain't it? Don't I have a say on who stays here or not?"

The sheriff, getting a little annoyed with the clerk, gave him a hard look, "I said give the man a room! Now! Before I haul you off to jail for disturbing the peace. Tom, you're wearing my skin mighty thin at the moment, always judging people by their looks and talking about a body behind their backs. I'm surprised people even stay here. Now, like I said, give the man a room!"

"Well, don't that beat all," he huffed but handed a key to Matt. "Here's a key to room #2. Would you please remove those spurs before climbing my stairs? We have a well-maintained place here, and I do hope you take that bath before you lay down on the bed. We'll have your bath ready in about fifteen minutes."

Matt was smiling as he accepted the key from the defeated desk clerk, then he turned to the sheriff.

"I reckon I'm obliged to you Sheriff, but I can't blame this fella too much. I can smell myself, and Tom, was it?" As he turned back to face the clerk, "I'm not a trouble maker, but I've been known not to run from it either. If the sheriff had his skin rubbed thin, then mine must be ready to rip right clean through." Turning back to the sheriff, he said, "Sheriff, I'm mighty sorry I offended your delicate sense-abilities."

Looking at Matt, the sheriff could hardly contain his laughter as he held it in He thought to himself. "This stranger seems a friendly enough sort. Yet there appears to be a side of him that if pushed, he'd do a lot of shoving back.

"I'll just remove my spurs, grab my saddlebags and bid you gent's goodbye for now."

As Matt climbed the stairs, he stopped to ask the clerk about the dining room.

"Say, I almost forgot to ask. How's the grub? The stable man says it's the best around?"

"Miss Sally is a real excellent cook," answered Tom, a little friendlier. "Makes fresh pies and bread every day, lays down a real good steak too. You'll smell that bread in the morning. People come from miles around on Sundays for her Sunday specials".

Matt was real happy to hear that. Nothing set his taste buds tingling like excellent home cooking.

"Thanks, Tom, is it? That's right kind of you to let me know. I'll be waiting on that bath and change into something clean, before heading for that grub".

Once Matt was in his room, as he opened a window to let some fresh air in, his mind went back to another town in Kansas. Dodge City, for years the only town on the frontier where all the buffalo hunters sold their pelts. A wide open town, noisy and always dangerous. A gun fight could break out at the drop of a hat, and it wasn't uncommon for someone to get a knife in the back over the money he was stupid enough to brag about. Once the buffalo herds began to thin out due to overhunting, the Plains Tribes began to get ornery, and war broke out. Matt thought about how the Army had such a hard time with the Cheyenne and the Kiowa. No sooner did they get them settled down than the Apache took to the warpath.

Matt became a scout after the Sioux got into the fracas. At every turn, the Sioux had the Army out-foxed.

Once the battle at the Little Big Horn took place, it all but spelled the end for the Sioux. The Army never beat the Sioux, they starved them into making peace. Now all the great buffalo herds were gone, and this town sat on one of the biggest hunting grounds for the tribes.

Chapter Two

Peace had prevailed on the Plains since the Indian wars ended and all the tribes were now on reservations. New regulations were rolling in each day from Washington, and the Army was being relieved of command of the tribes, and it was turned over to the bureau of Indian affairs. The terms of the treaties weren't being followed, and the way for the Indian seemed to obey or starve.

Most of the old War Chiefs were either dead or in prison, and the different bands of the Sioux looked for guidance from the new leaders. Some were content with staying the course and keeping the peace while others grew more and more difficult for the Indian Agents to handle. The council fires and spirit praying became more and more frequent, and there were rumors that the Indians were talking about leaving the reservations.

The treaty allowed the Dakota Sioux and its band's exclusive rights to the Black Hills with the agreement that no white man or the Army would step foot in the Black Hills.

The Lakota Sioux consisting of Sicangu, Oglala, Itazipco, Hunkpapa and the Miniconjou were sent further south to the barren and wasted plains while the Dakota had plenty of game to hunt with abundant pole pine to make shelters.

The Lakota had to depend on the agreements in the treaty which left them far short of their food allotments, clothing, and building materials. The Great Chief of the Lakota, Buffalo Robes grew more and more impatient with the new and corrupt Department of Indian Affairs.

Young upstarts that had never been to the war grew up hearing the legends of their elders were growing increasingly impatient with their leaders. They wanted to live as the elders had, free to roam the plains and hunt and live free. The only thing stopping them was the Tribal Council.

Even as Chiefs they didn't have the power to take the Nation to war. Being a chief was an honor, but the real power was held by the Nation's Council.

However, getting the whole council's decision was almost impossible now since the Sioux Nation had been divided up with part of the Nation residing in the Black Hills.

Corruption was deeply seated in the newfound agency, and the Lakota had no way to protest. At least with the Army, they had a say, even if it was just a little say. At least the Army would listen. This corruption left the Indians with no recourse but to either stay and starve or leave and revert back to their old ways.

So, Buffalo Robes, leading his people, left the reservation. He wasn't looking for a fight, he only wanted to lead them to their old hunting grounds. The plan was simple, wait until the annual dust storms that always came to the barren reservation. This was where the band was told to plant their corn and other vegetables.

It took months to make the weapons they would need and hide them from the reservation agent. Runners were sent to tell the other bands of the Plains, and now the only thing to do was wait for word that all were prepared and wait for the storms to cover their trail.

Buffalo Robes was an astute leader, and the Army viewed him as a formidable enemy, so much so that the only person who could make peace and bring the bands in, was Head Scout Matt Hutchins.

So it was on a moonless night, with the winds and dust blowing, that the great Chief Buffalo Robes took his people and left the reservation.

John D. Fie Jr

Chapter Three

Meanwhile, at headquarters, the rumors of the Sioux discontent weren't being taken seriously until the dispatch riders began to report in.

"Jumping frogs on a leaf," the Sergeant Major sang out when he opened the first dispatch of the day.

"Major, we got some trouble now!"

Seeing how excited the Sergeant was, the Major was eager to learn about the dispatch.

"Let me see that telegram, Sergeant." As he read the dispatch, the Major's face became grave, and the thought that at least one band had left the reservation.

"It doesn't say which band, Sergeant!"

"It's Buffalo Robes, Sir." The Sergeant answered.

Not being a veteran of the last Indian uprising, the Major didn't readily realize how serious this could be.

"Buffalo Robes, he's a sly one," said the Sergeant. "We never did beat him. It was Matt brought him in."

Confused now, the Major was looking for answers. "Who by George, is this Matt? Are you standing there telling me the U.S. Cavalry couldn't beat this simple Savage and one man, this Matt brought him in?"

The Sergeant was ready to explain everything when another dispatch rider busted through the door, out of breath and looking very excited.

"I'll take that soldier," the Major ordered. As he read this second dispatch, it dawned on him that he had a severe problem. One which he wasn't ready for and had no experience in handling.

"Tell me soldier, which band is this?" the Major asked as he crumpled the dispatch in his hand.

"Black Elk, Sir," answered the soldier.

"Point out their last location on the map," ordered the Major.

The soldier pointed to a spot on the map to the west of their present location.

The Major begins to speak out loud, "So if Buffalo Robes was last seen here and Black Elk here, which way would you say they're headed, Sergeant?"

Looking at the map, the Sergeant studies it for a while. "Sir, from where both bands are, they're hundreds of miles apart and at least a thousand more to the Black Hills, that is, if that's where they're headed. The way I see it, sir, they may hook up. But, if I may suggest Sir, I'd wait for the other dispatch riders to report in."

"But suppose both bands are heading for the Black Hills?" Looking at the map more, the Major decides it might be a good idea to send out patrols, one going straight west and one to the southeast. Turning he said, "How many scouts do we have at our disposal, Sergeant?"

Not liking the question, the Sergeant tells him, "All scouts have been discharged, except for one, Chief Scout Matt Hutchins and he's not likely to go searching out the Sioux."

"I see." said the Major. Looking at the map again the Major makes the decision to send out two troops without scouts. "We'll wait until the other dispatches arrive, then inform Washington."

The Sergeant Major knew only too well sending out two troops of Cavalry to search out Buffalo Robes, and Black Elk was a waste of time, but then, only time would tell depending on the other dispatches. Having a commanding officer with no experience in Indian affairs and no field experience, there'd be a massacre, especially up against Buffalo Robes. All the dispatches were in by noon, and three more bands had left the reservation. An estimated 5 to 6,000 Indians on the loose. Men, women, and children all headed somewhere.

However, all this activity painted a better picture of the situation. There was no mistake now that the Sioux were all going to join up someplace, but where?

The Sergeant Major reported to his commander. "The rest of the dispatches are in Major, three more bands are on the move, Sir."

The Major appears to be in deep thought as he paces back and forth. Looking out the window, he says somewhat excited, "Get a telegram off to Washington, Sergeant. Inform them of the situation. Also, send out telegrams for this Matt Hutchins. Every post on the frontier should be alerted to the present situation and be on the lookout for both Hutchins and the renegades. I want patrols sent out in every direction until we locate their position. Also, send out telegrams to all towns in every direction, maybe your Mr. Hutchins can be found in one of them."

John D. Fie Jr

Chapter Four

After enjoying a long bath and a hot meal, all Matt wanted was sleep. After a restful night, with the morning sun coming through the windows, Matt woke with the realization that a new day had dawned and what a difference it was to sleep in bed with sheets, pillow, and real blankets, waking with no aches or pains to begin the day. Searching through his saddlebags, he found a fresh shirt. As Matt dressed, his thoughts make him laugh at himself, as Matt thinks about civilization. He wonders if getting older is making him soft. But then hunger gets the best of him. He straps on his 45's, and he's out the door heading for the dining room for breakfast.

As he enters the dining room, all eyes are on him as he searches out a table with a view of both the door and the street.

History and learned lessons of survival have taught him to never leave his back exposed. Finding a spot in a far corner, Matt removes his hat and sits. It didn't take long for word to get around that the stranger in town was now in the dining room. A crowd began to gather outside, more out of curiosity than anything else.

As the waitress makes her way over to Matt, she looks out at all the onlookers. "Sir, you do know how to attract attention, don't you?"

Matt smiles at her and thinks he has to agree with her. It happens every time he goes into a town or settlement. Even more so in the towns that have sprung up in the past three or four years since the Indians have been on the reservations.

The westward move was bringing more and more people from all walks of life, some with money to build towns and stores. The biggest move was the railroad link between the East and the West. So in all the areas where Matt had once roamed free, he found were built up whenever he passed through. He looked up at the waitress as she asked, "What will it be Mister?"

The answer to her question was in her hand. The coffee pot! Matt turned up a cup and pointed.

The waitress smiled as did Matt. She asked, "So you're also a man without words as well as being great at gathering crowds."

Matt was taken in by her pleasant smile and sense of humor and laughed, "Not really, Ma'am just seems to happen naturally like."

As she took in his manner and the way he was dressed, she said, "I see you're not one for crowds and towns, probably don't like people either?" Looking up, Matt just smiles and points again to the cup for a refill.

"This sure is good coffee, Ma'am," he told her. "I'll have the eggs, bacon and some flap-jacks Ma'am." He smiles again and watches as she walks away to place the order. Not watching where she's going, she bumps into the mayor and spills coffee on his freshly cleaned suit.

"Sally! What in blue blazes are you doing?" yelled the mayor. "Just look at me!"

The mayor, now noticing Matt, "Well," he exclaimed. "I can see what the entire ruckus is about. You, sir, are a disturbance."

"That's just your opinion," Matt pointed to the crowd outside, "don't seem to mind me one bit."

Matt enjoys every minute of the situation as not one person in town has any idea of his name, let alone who he is. The one place where they usually got this kind of information was no help because the hotel clerk didn't get the name of the stranger.

"And pray tell, what is your name, Sir?" The mayor demanded, "And who are you? I've gotten reports about you disturbing the peace since you got here. Someone get the sheriff in here, we'll soon get to the bottom of this."

Leaving the mayor standing there with no answers, Matt's breakfast arrived, and he began eating without looking up or giving an answer.

The mayor started to say something then turned as he heard a voice.

"Can't you people leave this man alone for one minute," he growled looking directly at the mayor. "Any of you? Now get moving." The sheriff was having a bad day, not only was folks badgering him about the stranger, but one of the ranchers had just reported rustling of some of his cattle. The town couldn't afford to hire deputies so he would have to go it alone, leaving the town unattended.

"Mayor," the sheriff said, "We've got more pressing problems then this stranger, which by the way ain't causing no trouble."

The mayor glared at the sheriff. "Just what other trouble would that be, Sheriff?"

Matt sat calmly listening to all this and thinking this mayor is the reason I don't care much for towns.

"Rustlers and I got no deputies," the sheriff answered.

"We shouldn't discuss this here, Sheriff," the mayor exclaimed. "Let's go to my office."

Matt was becoming extremely irritated by now. "Hey! Let me eat in peace, would you? In other words, leave!"

Both the mayor and sheriff turn and look at Matt. The sheriff again laughs softly. There's something about this stranger that he likes, but can't figure it out yet.

The two men left the café and started down the street. They began a discussion about the problem of rustlers showing up now.

"Sheriff! Sheriff! Hold up!" The telegraph operator, out of breath, hands a telegram to the sheriff. "This just came over the wire, Sheriff."

The sheriff took the paper and opened it, "Oh boy. More problems." The sheriff handed the telegram to the Mayor. The mayor reads it and almost faints.

"What are we going to do Sheriff?" asked the mayor. "Surely the Indians aren't your problem Sheriff."

The mayor handed the telegram back to the sheriff and asked, "This stranger. This Matt Hutchins, is he an outlaw?"

The sheriff takes back the telegram, looks it over again and says. "I don't think he's an outlaw. The Army's looking for him to scout for them. But I've got to have some deputies. The Indians jumping the reservations is Army business, and we should keep tight lipped about it for now. The rustlers are what I got to deal with now, and I need to do it soon!"

The mayor nods toward the hotel. "I think your answer for a deputy is over in that dining room. There ain't nobody else in town that's got the makings of a deputy."

The sheriff removes his hat, wipes his face on his sleeve, looks at the hotel, and then turns to the telegraph operator. "Pete, send out a wire and get me a description of this Matt Hutchins."

"Right away Sheriff," the operator said. "Where will you be when an answer comes back?"

"You just find me no matter where I'm at and get that wire out without giving out any information to anyone, understand? Especially about the Indians leaving. We need to keep all this close to our chests for the time being, at least until we know more. Now, if you two will excuse me, I've got business to attend to."

He placed his hat back on his head and headed across the street in the direction of the hotel, then he turns abruptly toward the livery stable.

Clem, seeing the sheriff heading his way is all smiles and spits out a bit of his chew.

"Took you long enough to git here. Want to take a look see at that fella's Hoss, don't ya?" Clem asked excitedly. "Well, let me tell you, that their Hoss is as strange looking' as its owner. It's all painted up with those Injun markings. I ain't never seen the like. Injun markings on his Hoss, Injun blanket, and Army saddle. All dressed up in buckskins. You know he won't give a fella a straight answer."

"Clem," the sheriff interrupted, "never mind all you're mumbling, just show me the horse. I swear you're like an old woman sometimes, ranting and rambling and babbling on and on. A person would think you were kin to Tom over at the hotel."

"I ain't no kin to that noisy smooth talking city slicker," Clem fussed. "I hear'd tell he insulted that stranger and with all this Injun stuff and markings, I wouldn't be at all surprised to find out the stranger scalped that fool. Here's his Hoss, strange looking ain't he?"

If the sheriff hadn't seen it, he wouldn't have believed it. Here in Buffalo Flats. With a surprised look on his face, he stands up straight and looks at Clem.

"Know who he is, Sheriff? Strange looking ain't it? Take a look-see at this." He lifted a rear hoof and showed the sheriff. "See that. They're Army shoes. Yes sir, strange, mighty strange."

Knowing how Clem likes to gossip, the sheriff decides to keep what he's thinking to himself.

"Never mind Clem," he told him. "I don't want to hear about you babbling all over town about this fella, you understand?" He turned and started walking away, then turned back, "If anybody's looking for me, I'll be over at the café having a coffee."

When he walks in, he sees that Matt is still at the same table, still eating. "Mind I sit down?" as he stands in front of Matt.

Matt nods to a chair. "Sure, sit."

Grabbing a chair, the sheriff sits across from the stranger. "Time to fess up partner," the sheriff says, "you got the town in an uproar. The mayor tells me you're a disturbance. Clem tells me you're strange, and those folks outside are looking at you like you belong in a museum. I don't care which. But I need to ask, how long you staying with us?"

"Well to answer one question, not long and the other question, why is it so dang important for everybody to know my name?"

Usually, when Matt gave his name trouble started, from him being called a half-breed to being a savage and a lot of other things. There had been many men that had felt Matt's anger and many a battle has been fought as a result of that violence.

The sheriff handed Matt the telegram and asks, "Any idea who this fellow is? I checked the rig on that Roan of yours. There's only one man on the frontier rides a Roan like that. Right, Matt?"

Matt noticed the smile on the sheriff's face, "Took you long enough," and smiled himself.

"Look here, Matt," said the sheriff as he leaned across the table. "I've got trouble here.

Indians leaving the reservation and now rustlers. The Indians ain't really my problem. That's what we got the Army for. My trouble is the rustlers, and I need a tracker. What do you say?"

Matt's thoughts were pointed in two directions. The Army and now the sheriff. The Army came. First, he was, after all, Chief of Scouts. Rustlers were not all that much of a problem, and Matt's thoughts seemed to be in one direction on this question. This whole thing could be one problem.

"Seems strange Sheriff, the Sioux jumping the reservations and you missing cows. Could be one in the same." The sheriff's face broke into a smile, realizing Matt might have given him the answer to his dilemma.

"You know when they left the reservation. You got any idea?"

"No, this telegram doesn't say when. By the way, the Army's looking for you."

"You understand that I'll have to get going to find where they're headed. Also, I need to see if the Sioux truly are the ones doing the rustling. I've got a feeling they ain't, but I want to be sure about it. You need to understand, if we do pick up a trail and find out it's not the Sioux, I'll have to Part Company and find them before the shooting starts, and people get killed. That's all we need out here at this time, another war.

Chapter Five

After discussing the matter, Matt asked the sheriff to send a telegram to the Army at Fort Kearny and notify them that he'll start looking for the Sioux. "Convince the Army that you need my help right now more than they do. We'll head out in the morning and start trailing where the cows are missing."

Two patrols returned to the Fort empty handed and needed to resupply.

"Sergeant Major," one of the soldiers said, "It's like they just disappeared, no trace of 'me anywhere."

The Indian agent reported that all week the drums had been going, and when he went out to check each morning, nothing seemed to be wrong until he went out one morning and they were all gone. They had just disappeared as if into thin air."

The Sergeant Major wasn't surprised to hear this because it was a trick that Buffalo Robes had pulled many times, using the dust storms to cover all their tracks. "That Indian may be old, but by golly, he still thinks the same."

"Has anyone found this Matt Hutchins? Where in tarnation is he?" The Sergeant Major looks at the Major and shrugs his shoulders.

"My god man! Is he a ghost? Is there any word from Washington yet? How the blazes do they expect me to track down 6,000 Indians in this wilderness with only four troops at my disposal? Is there any word from Fort Kearny?"

Four days pass, and there was still no trace of Buffalo Robes and Black Elk. Dispatch riders came in every day with the same reports, no sightings. Plus there wasn't any word on the whereabouts of Matt Hutchins. Nine outposts and no word or any good news to report.

"Major, this telegram just arrived from Fort Kearny. It's Hutchins, Sir. They've located him in Buffalo Flats."

"Where is Buffalo Flats, Sergeant Major?" He looked over the map.

Sergeant Major moves around the desk, points to a spot. "I figured he'd go back there. He was raised there by the Sioux. There's a mesa called the Enchanted Mesa where he finds solitude."

Because of his upbringing, the Major was amazed that a white man could or would be raised by savages.

"What else do I need to know about this man, Sergeant?"

The Sergeant Major hesitated to tell the Major that there were reports of Blackfeet Army Scouts being killed and scalped. The Sergeant knew who was doing it, as long as there was one Blackfoot, there would always be war.

"It says here Sergeant that they've been finding some dead Army Scouts. I thought you told me we had no Scouts?"

The Sergeant searches for the right words, but could only say, "They were Scouts from Fort

Kearny. Washington kept them there. All the outposts weren't required to have scouts."

"It also says," the Major read, "that this Hutchins is in Buffalo Flats asking to start his search from there, something about rustlers." He looked at the map once more trying to figure out why this Hutchins would begin there. The Sergeant made the suggestion, "Maybe he feels they might be heading in that direction."

The next morning's dispatch brought answers to some of the questions. A patrol from one of the furthest outposts failed to return, and another patrol was being sent to find them.

"This could be real bad news, Major," said Sergeant Major. "That patrol was ordered to search the southeast. That could have put them between both bands or at least close to one of them. In either case, Matt could maybe be on the right track."

The Major started pacing again. It was a habit he had when he was thinking hard.

"You may be right, Sergeant, but looking at the map, why in thunders Gulch, would the Indians be going that way? The Black Hills are way up here," he pointed to the map, "to the northeast? Send a telegram and find out if there have been any reports of trouble up there. This might be a diversion to throw us off track, and have the bugler sound officer's call."

Usually, Officer's Call never took place at any outpost, so not being used to it, a lot of officers arrived late and out of uniform.

"Gentlemen," the Major began, "I know this assembly is a bit unusual, but being out of uniform is not acceptable! Some of you are aware that the Sioux have left the reservations. Probably close to 6,000 are on the loose. This presents us with a problem, and we must pay utmost attention to regulations for all our safety and turn this command into a fit fighting outfit. Have your troopers check their equipment, replace what needs to be replaced, then have them ready for boots and saddles. You. Artillery officers, prepare your guns and make sure there's plenty of ammunition. This may turn into a long campaign, so load the supply wagons. Are there any questions?"

One young officer had a question, "Sir, are you actually planning to bring along field guns?"

An older seasoned Captain added. "The guns may slow the column down, there is some rough terrain out there, Sir."

"Are you questioning my orders, Captain? I'm aware of your brilliant war record, and your experience with these savages, but once we've caught up with them, it's my intention to end it once and for all. Teach them a lesson they won't soon forget. Do I make myself clear on this, Gentlemen?"

All heads nodded in agreement except one. The Captain thinks to himself, *this is going to be a foolhardy march.*

"Then," the Major shouted, "With all in agreement, you are dismissed."

The Sergeant Major joins the Captain. "You've got to excuse the Major, Captain. He doesn't realize the danger in all this. It's Buffalo Robes and Black Elk themselves, Captain. That's Matt Hutchins' people we're going after, and the Major sent for Hutchins himself to scout."

The Captain kicks the dirt, then glanced at the Sergeant Major. "Buffalo Robes and Black Elk are a hand full on the reservation, and now out there on their own terrain. Why those field guns will be worthless if we get into a fight with them. You know, Sergeant Major, as well as I do, those two Chiefs aren't going to challenge us to head on. They'll go about it in their own way, and those big guns are just extra baggage. My god, Sergeant Major, when Hutchins lays eyes on those weapons, the Major will be dealing with his anger, and we both know how that can be like."

The Sergeant Major nodded in agreement. He knew full well that Matt wasn't going to approve the use of artillery. He looked to the Captain and shrugged his shoulders.

"I've known him since the last surrender when we realized he was a white captive, at least we thought so. They shipped him back east to St. Louis to a mission school. He stayed just long enough to learn to speak English and then he took off. I run into him a few years back when we needed a scout to track down the Apaches. Those guns were used on an Apache village, killing women and children and Matt went wild. He ain't gonna lead this group nowhere near those Sioux, not if the Major is planning on using those guns.

Chapter Six

Just before daybreak, Matt was saddled and ready, waiting in front of the sheriff's office. The thought of being corralled into this was an unwanted venture. Here he was going out to find the very people who raised him, taught him how to live and survive. It was sickening, but he also thought if he could talk to them first, maybe he could convince them to give it up and go back to the reservation, without bloodshed.

"There you are, Sheriff. I'd just about give up on you. Looks like you might've had too much town life."

Sheriff Fry moaned and glared at Matt, then moans again. "It's been years since I got up this early." If he were going to be riding with Matt, he would have to get used to early hours and no breakfast, not to mention plenty of long hours in the saddle.

"Let's move out," Matt said and started 'Ole Friend down the street. If they were gonna find these rustlers quick, they had to go before the trail got too cold.

"We'll head west and then north to the river," Fry explained. "That's where the tracks ended, so the ranchers couldn't follow any further."

It didn't take long to get to the spot so Matt could do his work. He knew exactly where he wanted to start. The old buffalo watering hole.

"That's kind of rough country for cattle Sheriff," he said. "Instead of going west, then north we'd be better off heading northwest to the end of the canyon. If that's the way they went, we should be able to pick up the trail on that soft ground. We could cut a day of tracking in that rough country instead of taking the chance of having one of the horses going lame, throwing a shoe, or worse yet, get caught in an ambush in the canyon."

"You're right Matt. If we got ambushed in that canyon, it'd be bad for our health. You're the tracker do it your way?"

As they head northwest, Fry was thinking how lucky he was to have Matt Hutchens to track these rustlers. Secretly he was hoping the rustling wasn't being done by the Sioux.

"Gonna is dark soon," Matt told him. "There's a waterhole just north of here, so we'll make camp and get an early start at first light. You're looking like you're bone tired and saddle sore."

Sheriff Fry said, "I was just about to ask where we were gonna camp. "It's been quite a spell since I rode this far in a day.

Matt wasn't used to riding with anyone and Fry recognized that fact. Matt could tell he was only trying to make conversation. All Matt would do was nod his head in agreement

"It's beautiful country at that. There was a time, though when all you could see was Buffalo way over to the horizon. I haven't been in these parts for a spell, and I still can't believe all the settling that people are doing out here. I just hope those Sioux don't run into anybody that could spell trouble. A huge problem."

The Lakota knew about the Waseca (white man) who were scouting for the Army and reporting back about how many there were. But they found no sign of the Alicia (soldiers). Hearing this information, Buffalo Robes decided to gather his sub-band leaders and hold council on what they should do next. After a long council meeting, they decided to send out a party to find Black Elk and his people and tell him of the change in plans. The original plan was to have all the bands meet on the hunting grounds at the Mesa then continue on to the northwest into the mountains. Then they would go on to the land of the Queen mother.

Buffalo Robes called all the people together to let everybody know about the change in plans. He noticed the disappointment in their eyes and heard the muffled talk. Everyone was looking forward to meeting their friends at the hunting grounds to hunt buffalo and fill their bellies. Now, however, because of the whites, there were no Buffalo, and there would be no hunt.

The young Braves were disappointed and angry, not being able to hunt like their forefathers. They had heard many great stories growing up listening to the stories of the elders. These stories made the young bucks anxious to put fear into the white eyes because they had taken their lands away and made the buffalo disappear.

Chapter Seven

Buffalo Robes, up to his old tricks, sent out several packs of warriors in different directions, telling them to leave plenty sign to hopefully confuse anybody that was tracking them. The Warriors had orders not to fight and to leave as many tracks and signs as possible. However, one of the parties ran into an Army patrol just south of the main body. They rode north, and they ran into one another.

The Calvary was young, inexperienced and spoiling for their first fight. The Indians had a mixture of experienced fighters and young bucks who were eager to prove themselves to the tribe. The fight was short lived as the Calvary was outnumbered two to one. The new Officer led the troops into a full charge with sabers drawn. The

Warriors took the high ground and waited for the attacking soldiers to break and try to climb up. As soon as they broke up, the horses were winded, and now they started the climb. The War Chief signaled the Braves to attack the troopers. They took the soldiers by surprise by charging down the hill as some of the troopers tried to dismount and fight on the ground. The orders to dismount came too late. By the time they had tried to dismount, the Lakota were cutting them to pieces. The troopers who had dismounted were being overrun by the Braves with their lances. Now with the Lakota in close, the trooper's sabers were of no use, and it became hand to hand fighting.

The young Lieutenant gave a gallant try, but to no avail. He went down with a lance to the throat. As he lay on the ground, struggling to breathe, blood pouring from his mouth, a brave struck him with a tomahawk, then took his hair. The only living soldiers were the wounded, and the Lakota started scalping. Some soldiers were scalped while still alive and the bodies stripped of their uniforms. The Braves, grabbing uniforms, weapons, horses, anything that could be useful, headed back to the tribe. The Braves were triumphal with the way the battle went. On the ride back, there was much bragging. They didn't realize what they had done would anger Buffalo Robes. Even though they felt they had no choice when they ran into the troops, Buffalo Robes' orders were to make tracks, leave a sign and avoid any fighting. Now, soldiers were dead, scalps were taken, and the Chief knew this would mean only one thing in the eyes of the white eyes. War!

As the Braves rode into camp, the people started chanting and praising as they saw the many scalps and the clothes of the soldiers. Then they heard the voice of Buffalo Robes, the people knew he was angry by his loud voice. On this day, many young braves would feel the wrath of their Chief.

Buffalo Robes ordered that all horse's hooves to be wrapped in cloth, then braves were sent out to bring brush to sweep away all signs they might leave. The Chief felt that it was vital to join up with Black Elk, so together they would be stronger, and the Army would have trouble trying to bring them all back. Every person in both bands was determined not to return to the reservation. If they were to die then let it be in their own lands, they would reclaim. It might seem an impossible dream, but the people believed this dream was something they would fight for to the end.

Matt and Fry came upon some strange looking tracks on the second day that didn't look like Sioux tracks.

"Sheriff," said Matt, "something's wrong with the signs here. I can't put my finger on it, but the Sioux would never do something like this."

Fry had never seen Indian tracks before, so he said to Matt, "I got to go along with you. After all, you're the one with experience, not me."

"We'll go a little further on and make camp up in the tree line, hunt something to eat then get another early start in the morning."

As the sun made its journey out of sight behind the horizon, Matt could see that Fry was as tired as the horses if not more so.

"See those tracks," Matt pointed. "There's been people here before. See that clearing? Shod horses, not Indian ponies."

"Whoever it was used unshod horses to make the trail hard to follow, or they were trying to make it look like Indians. See how they're strung out over here. Had to be a Ramada. There's no way Indians would make tracks like this."

"Well," exclaimed Fry. "That clears up part of the mystery. Now we have to find out who."

"We'll pitch camp over there in that underbrush, not here in the open," Matt told him. "You gather some dry wood, and I'll go set up a rabbit snare."

They sat around after eating and tried to figure out the signs. However putting the pieces together wasn't easy, not without more signs and a place where someone could take the cattle.

"I know where they're going," said Matt excitedly. "The Army Post twenty to thirty miles west. There's water in between. I'm willing to bet if we scout the western end of this canyon we'll find a sign of those cattle. There's an Army outpost not far to the west. All their provisions are freighted in, and fresh beef would be hard to get. It would be the perfect place to sell your stolen cattle. They've got a quarter-master and a telegraph. When you get back to town, send a wire and see if they need any more meat. You may get the answer you're looking for."

Fry asked, "How many outposts are out here?"

"Don't know exactly. There are about thirty to fifty miles apart, stretching, across the territory. The

Army got a real scare with the last uprising when they faced Sitting Bull and Crazy Horse, so they broke up the tribes and sent them to different reservations, and they put outposts to guard them."

"Didn't know that. I don't get out of town much anymore. Nothing seems to happen in town, except for a few drunks on payday shooting up the place and getting into fights."

"Sounds like a real exciting life, Sheriff. I don't reckon a little action ever hurt nobody, at least every once in a while."

"I'll take the quiet little peaceful town after dealing with some of those cow towns in Kansas. Thank you, very much," said Sheriff Fry.

"I'm tuckered out, and I know your bones are. What do you think we call it a day? We're gonna be getting up early."

Fry didn't say anything, just nodded and rolled over.

Fry awoke to the smell of brewing coffee, "You're sure an early bird! It's still dark. However, I got to admit that coffee sure smells good. You know I had a hard time getting to sleep. I laid there thinking about the people in town. Not many of them leave, except for the bank president. He's always going on business trips, but I doubt he'd have anything to do with all this rustling. He's been foreclosing on farmers when they had a bad crop and fire destroyed one man's crop. I'm glad he leaves town for a while because when he's there, he gets together with the mayor, and they give me a massive headache."

"I was gonna ask you if the mayor was always such a pain." I feel sorry for you having to deal with folks like him.

Both The Sheriff and Matt rolled and enjoyed their smoke while drinking their coffee. When they finished up and were in the saddle following the hoof prints leading toward the canyon. They were almost to the entrance of the canyon when they heard shots. Both men rolled out of their saddle's, hitting the ground and hurrying behind a big rock.

"Did you see where those shots came from?" Fry asked Matt.

Without answering the Sheriff, Matt began working his way up the side of the rocky overhang.

It looked like that was more than likely where the shooter was located. He gave the sheriff a couple hand signals motioning for him to stay put. Matt found the spot he was looking for and motioned for the sheriff to open fire. Immediately return fire was coming down.

One of the ambushers said to his partner, "I kin only see one of 'me. Where you think, the other one is?"

"I don't know! You just keep your dang eyeballs peeled for him. He's down there somewhere, and you need to make sure he don't circle around behind us."

"You think I should move to get a better shot?"

The man never heard his partner's answer because he was hit by a round from Matt's Sharps rifle. His lifeless body landed just a few inches from his friend.

"Virgil, I swear," as he looked at his partner's dead body, the blood seeping into the dirt, "you went and done got yourself kilt." Half out of his mind the man began to get careless, and Matt's rifle took off half his head, and he fell dead next to his friend.

"That was some mighty fine shooting," exclaimed the sheriff as he stood up from behind the rock. "I heard those Sharps rifles was powerful, but by golly, they beat a pistol something fierce."

"You ever see these two before?" Matt asked.

Fry was digging through their pockets, stood and shook his head, "Don't recognize either of them. Ain't nothing on them to tell who they are? Don't recall flyers on them either. Let's mount up and look for their horses. Maybe there's something in their saddle bags.

They hadn't ridden far when Matt said, "There. That cut away in the rocks. More than likely it's their camp. Be careful. There could be more."

They searched the area and found the horses behind some brush. Fry dismounted and walked to the horses. Searching the saddlebags, he turned to Matt. "Nothing in them to tell any more than we already know. I don't recognize the brand on these horses either. Looks like we still got nothing to help us."

"I'll scout down the canyon and see what I can find. Meanwhile, you strip the horses and cut them loose. We'll cut the head off the fella, and you can take back to town. Maybe somebody can identify it."

Matt riding slow and easy searched every bit of ground watching carefully for any sign. He didn't find anything. No hoof prints of either horses or cattle so continued on to the end of the canyon where the owl-hoots had been camped. Finding nothing, he headed back up the canyon.

As he turned 'Ole Friend, he spotted something on the ground. He got down and picked up a conch, either from a gun belt, a hat, or possibly a vest. With something like this, all the sheriff had to do was find the owner of this conch. That should be an easy task in a small town like Buffalo Flats.

"Matt! Over here!" Yelled the sheriff as Matt came into view. "Have a look at this hoof print. I know at least, I'm fairly sure I've seen it before. Seems to me it was at Clem's livery stable." Matt dismounted, inspected the hoof prints, and then hands the conch to the sheriff.

"Shouldn't be too hard for you to match up this conch with somebody in town. Should be easy to spot a missing conch."

Matt turned back to look closer at the hoof prints. "Look here," he pointed at the points. "See that bar? I saw Clem putting shoes a bay mare when I came into town. I think it belonged to the livery stable."

Fry smiled at Matt, "With this conch and those hoof prints maybe we're gitting closer to finding out something. I'm glad I don't have that head back in the saddle bag."

"I didn't say you didn't have to take the head back. Don't let your delicate sense-abilities keep you from doing what needs to be done. Get over there and get to cutting. The sooner you start, the sooner you'll be done. Just call it more evidence for the people to identify."

Glancing up at the buzzards in the sky, Fry said, "I reckon the least we can do is bury what's left of these two." He points to the heavens, "Those birds think its dinner time."

Matt grins at Fry and says, "You mean to tell me you'd leavened hungry? I wonder about you, Sheriff.

Leave them yahoos right where they're at. They weren't nothing but varmints themselves. You do realize if it was you laying there, they sure as shooting wouldn't bury you."

Matt scouted around while the sheriff went to work with the bodies. Reckon you'll be heading back to town with your findings now?" He rode up to the sheriff who was fastening his saddle bag. "I need to find Buffalo Robes before any blood gets spilled. You figure you can handle all this?"

"You're not coming back to town with me?" asked Fry. "I know somebody that might not be jubilant if I come alone. Besides, I need someone to share this gruesome sight with me. I'm not looking forward to all the horrified looks when they see this head."

"Sheriff, all you got to do is tell that hotel fella that I'll miss him too. I got to get on the trail and find those Indians. I have to try and head them off. There's got to be a good reason why they just up and left the reservation. I'll ease back your way when I'm done with this.

"I wasn't talking about the hotel clerk, Matt, he's that way with everyone. No, the one I was talking about is Miss Sally. Seems to me she took a shining to you."

"Well, don't that beat all? I admit she's a mighty fine cook. I'll keep what you said in mind and ease back into town when I'm finished with this Indian business. You tell her if she seems upset, what I said, but don't you go embellishing any points in my favor, you hear?"

Mounting up, Matt touches the brim of his hat and gives a good hearty nod. "So long, for now, Sheriff."

John D. Fie Jr

Chapter Eight

Outposts all along the frontier readied themselves for the coming campaign. Patrols were sent out on five-day searches with orders to go in all directions with the thought that eventually one or more of the patrols would stumble on some sign of the fleeing Indians.

One patrol did stumble on the remains of the missing patrol.

"Troop halt!" was the order given. "Sergeant, have the patrol dismount and search for survivors." It was doubtful there were any. All the bodies had been stripped of clothing and weapons. The patrol's company banner was also missing.

Mother Nature had done her work, and the buzzards were still hanging around. The site was a horrible scene for the young troopers as it was their first look at the results of a battle. The reality of war was forever seared into their memory, and many lost their breakfast. All the rest of the day, no one mentioned a word about how easy it was going to be when they met up with the fleeing Indians. In truth, an awful fear was settling in amongst the young troopers.

As the dispatch rider arrived with the news of the massacre that took place, the Major read the dispatch and couldn't believe what he read.

"Those savages took all the uniforms and equipment, then scalped them. Sergeant Major, who or what are we dealing with here? Send a wire to

Fort Kearney with this news. We'll wait for their answer, then march at first light."

Fort Kearney's response wasn't very encouraging. Another troop had run into a band of hostiles only a few miles from the first massacre. How many bands were on the loose and were they all, Sioux? There were survivors this time to give a full report. There wasn't any doubt that both Black Elk and Buffalo Robes had been involved. This latest skirmish was indeed Black Elk, and his band was headed in the same direction as Buffalo Robes. With Black Elk and Buffalo Robes united, the whole tribe of the Lakota, which was separated after the last uprising, would now be back together with all the sub-bands joined as one. Both Chiefs were experienced and crafty. Along with the sub-bands and their leaders, they made a very formidable enemy.

Tracking to the southeast, Matt was sure he would cross paths with Buffalo Robes. He was determined to find them before the Calvary with the hope to avoid an all-out war. Matt was unaware of the fighting that had already taken place. He was confident he knew where they were headed. The valley to the North West had always been a good winter camp for the Lakota. They weren't aware of how much settling had taken place, and the head of the valley was just north of Buffalo Flats causing it to be in the middle of their flight north.

Matt picked up some tracks on the third day but became a little confused when he saw these tracks came from the opposite direction where

Buffalo Robes would be traveling. "So," he said to himself. "There are two bands, maybe more off the reservation." That would only mean one thing. All five bands would be on the move making up the whole Lakota tribe.

"There's no doubt 'Ole Friend," as Matt patted his horse's neck. "A fight's gonna take place. Looks like Buffalo Robes has had enough."

Giving 'Ole Friend his head they struck out at a faster lope. The trail was beginning to show recent signs and was easier to follow. They climbed a level rise to see the plains spread as far as the eye could see. He spotted a Calvary patrol off in the distance. "Let's join up with them, Friend, and get an idea of what's going on."

The Black Foot scouts guiding the Calvary had spotted Matt and 'Ole Friend. They reported to the Captain what they saw. As Matt drew close to the patrol, he spotted an old enemy from years past. A Black Foot scout by the name of Scar. He got the name after a fight with Pahaska in the last Sioux and Black Foot war. He rode out to intercept this Pahaska. "You no welcome here, Pahaska. You are no friend. You go." Scar was trying to intimidate Matt, by trying to keep him away from the patrol. He wanted to keep Matt from telling the Calvary about the Sioux.

"I suggest you move out of my way Scar or that one scar you've got will get some company," Matt told the man. 'Ole Friend began to prance as he felt the tension between the two adversaries. Scar made a bad mistake, taking his eyes off Matt to see how far the troop had moved. He had to make it look as if Matt was in the wrong and as he turned around, Matt's fist knocked him off his horse. Before he hit the ground, Matt leaped off his horse, and they began rolling around on the ground.

"Alright you two, break it up!" the Captain yelled. Matt and Scar were too involved to hear or pay attention. "Separate them," the Captain ordered two troopers. However, the troopers got knocked aside while Matt and Scar continued to fight. The Captain removed his firearm and fired into the air. The sound of the pistol got them to stop.

"What in blue blazes is going on here?" The Captain turned his full attention on Scar. Scar nodded at Matt, "No friend . . . Speak lies to pony soldier."

Matt removed his pistol and laid it up aside Scar's head, knocking the man to the ground and probably giving him another scar on the other side of his face.

"Hello Captain," said Matt as he holstered his weapon. "How are things?"

The Captain smiled at Matt and asked, "Just what do you and these Black Feet have against one another?"

Matt moved to the side as two Black Feet scouts picked up Scar and helped him away. "Not much, Captain. How many lies have these vultures told you about the Lakota? You do know they lie to the Army, figuring to gain an advantage over them and secretly hoping you'll wipe out the Sioux nation. Something they've been trying to do for years."

"Where do you think they're going?" he asked.

Standing beside 'Ole Friend, Matt laughed. "Now that they know I'm here they know the show is over. They'll more than likely head back to the rocks they crawled out from under and lick their wounds. When they've done that, they'll follow behind and try to catch me in the open to ambush me."

Matt glanced over at the troopers then asked the Captain, "You know how scared these fellows are, don't you?

"We came upon a massacre," he explained. "There was Nothing pretty about it. It spooked these young troopers. That was the worst one, then there was another, had a couple survivors. How many do you reckon are out there?"

Standing beside the Captain and looking across the plains, Matt said he could only guess. "This is just a guess, but I'd say the whole Lakota tribe."

Chapter Nine

Three days later Buffalo Robes and Black Elks joined up. The celebration lasted well into the night with friends and family seeing one another again after years of separation. Both Chiefs agreed that with the young warriors being so aggressive and getting into fights with the Army patrols there would surely be trouble. Because of these reckless acts, it was best that they join together. This move would assure they would be stronger and able to fight as a united tribe. However, with so many young and untested warriors and the elderly and children to protect, it was going to be an enormous undertaking. So, it was agreed that they would travel north into the lands of the Queen Mother.

They felt that once they crossed the border, they would be safe from the Army.

But getting there wasn't going to be easy. As the Sioux started to move North with that many people and horses kicking up dust, it was going to be easy for the Army to spot them from miles away. So, it was important to move at night, keeping everyone together and keep sending parties to search out Army patrols and any other dangers that would give away their whereabouts away. The rest stops would have to be cold stops without campfires because fires and smoke would surely give their location away.

Matt knew all the tricks of the Sioux. Looking at the Captain, he told him, "Keep moving in the way you're going. I'll join up with you in a few days."

"I demand you stay with the patrol," the Captain was adamant about it. But Matt was just as headstrong telling the Captain, "Stay on the alert Captain and keep the troopers aware that I might come back after dark. And I don't want my head blown off."

Matt picked up the trail and began following it. He moved 'Ole Friend into a ground covering canter as the trail started getting fresher. The tracks were heading in a North West direction, and the people in Buffalo Flats was right in their path.

"This is getting worse by the hour 'Ole Friend. We've got to catch up with them, and soon."

Riding in the dark was challenging, but doable and by morning, Matt was sure they were only a few hours ahead of him. "I guess we can stop here 'Ole Friend and rest a bit." 'Ole Friend stomped his hooves a bit, gave a little nicker telling Matt he was in complete agreement, then he began munching on what grass he could find.

Matt finding a comfortable spot, leaned against a tree and was asleep instantly. Friend's nickering awoke him. "Why are you making all that noise, Friend?"

He stood to have a look-see and could hear the sound of gunfire in the distance, "We need to find a spot and see what's going on." He mounted up giving 'Ole Friend his knee, they moved into a comfortable lope. They stayed in the gully until they come to a small rise. Stopping 'Ole Friend, he dismounts and climbs the rise on hands and knees. He removes his hat, raises his head and takes a quick look at what's going on.

In the distance, he could see a fight that made it clear that there was probably no chance of peace. From what he could see, the Sioux was getting the best of what looked to be a whole troop of Cavalry. He slid back down the rise, reached Friend and made the decision to join the battle, or he could wait and follow the survivors. It was a tough decision for him, but if he let the Sioux see him, maybe they would break off the fight.

It was a slim chance, but worth trying. He could give the sign and possibly get the fight to end. And hope the Cavalry wouldn't think he had anything to do with it.

Matt found a spot where the Indians could clearly see him. He had 'Ole Friend began to prance. It wasn't long before someone noticed Pahaska on the high ground. The Sioux stopped fighting, and the Cavalry stopped also. Cheers and shouts went up from the embattled Cavalry troop as the Sioux started riding toward Matt. As Buffalo Robes, led the war party away from the battlefield the Sioux were celebrating the appearance of Pahaska. Surely things would be alright now with Pahaska back among the people. The Braves were shouting all types of praise and joy.

Matt smiled and was happy to see those that he grew up with. They were older now and very lean from not getting enough to eat. Immediately Matt knew what was up as Buffalo Robes and Black Elk approached. He saw the grave look on Buffalo Robes' face. However, the look of Black Elk was one of joy. Black Elk acted sincerely as he shook hands with Matt, saying Ho-ha-he.

Buffalo Robes was more sincere in his greeting because he knew why Matt had come. He was aware that this time there would be no talk of peace. He said in the Lakota tongue, "Ah, my son, to only see you in the bad times and not the good."

Buffalo Robes knew the Army had sent Matt.

"My father," Matt said to him. "I understand there are no good times or you wouldn't have taken the people from the reservation and put yourself in great danger. The women look weak, and the young ones wear rags. Tell me, oh Great One, what has happened?" He knew it was a serious matter when he saw that the whole Lakota were together, with all the sub-bands and their leaders, assembled and ready for council.

Buffalo Robes took Matt aside and started to explain. "Many of the people have already gone to happy hunting ground to be with those who passed before them. The people have grown tired of lies told by the ones from the village of Washington. They tell us to plant the seeds they give us, but the ground does not like the seed. Nothing grows. The Wasicu (white man) say to the Lakota there will be much to eat, many blankets to keep warm when the cold winds come. All Lies! Spoken with forked tongues. The people go with empty bellies. The young ones cry from sickness, the old ones look to the heavens and want to see the old life once more before they leave us. This, my son, has made me think carefully. The pain in my heart for my people has helped me make a move to the winter camp in the mountains. There it is good hunting, plenty of lodge poles for shelter. To hunt once again for the Tatanka (buffalo). The people cry out for the old ways, the ways of the Lakota, not the ways of the Wasicu. We do not wish Ozuye (war) with the Milahanska (long knives) my son. We only want to live in peace, the Lakota way."

"We should sit with the others, my father, and smoke and speak. I've much to tell you." Matt was hoping that he could make some progress with all assembled at the council fire. But from the condition of the people and the mood of his father, it wasn't going to easy.

"Tonight we sit," Buffalo Robes told him. We speak, smoke and tell of old times, but for now my son, it makes me happy to see you once again. Your mother longs to see you and speak with you. Storm Women looks this way, and I see with my eyes the longing in her heart. Go to her. We will talk later.

"Ho-ha-he, ho-ha-he. My son." Storm Women came running to Matt with her arms wide open, grabbing him with a big hug. "It has been many moons since I have seen you last. Come, we will sit and talk."

"How have you been, Mother? I see that sad times have fallen on the people, but it makes me happy to see you in good spirits," said Matt, as they both sat before the fire. "I see much hunger Mother, on the young and the old. This is not okay."

"Yes my son, there is much hunger. Each day the warriors go out to hunt but return with nothing to fill the stomach. Many of the old go off to wait to cross over, to be with the Great Spirit. But let's not talk about the sadness. Let us talk about you. Have you a woman to warm your blankets? The name of Pahaska fills the talk of the young maidens. The young warriors speak of riding with you. Look. There is now much hope when they see you among the people. You bring much pride to your father's lodge."

"I come to visit and to talk with the council and ask them to return to the reservations. No good can come of this. There are too many whites, and I fear for the people." Storm Women listened as Matt spoke and when he had finished, he hoped that she knew why he had come, and maybe she could have a word with Buffalo Robes.

"My son," she said. "The people will not return. There is much sadness there, and the Army dishonors your father with their lies. They try to make slaves of the Lakota. They take our children and try to teach them the ways of the whites. When they took you away, it saddened my heart. So many of the young have heard of the old ways and long to live the way of the Lakota. Your father will never lead the people back into the ways of the whites. We do not wish to fight, but it has already started. There is too much talk of the great things before the bad times started. Of the many things that made Sitting Bull and Crazy Horse lead the Lakota to war. It was the hard times and the suffering of the people and the lies of the peace talks that put us in the wrong places called reservations. The Oglala and Hunk-Papa with the others will fight to the end. This, you must speak with your father."

Chapter Ten

Matt was summoned to join the circle and speak to the council. As Matt walked away, Storm Women thought back to the first day when Buffalo Robes brought the child to their lodge. Saddened by their loss at the birth of just two moons ago, the baby was thought to be a gift from the Great Spirit, to bring happiness once again into their lodge. Watching Matt grow honored both Buffalo Robes and Storm Women. He brought joy to all the people in the many fights with the enemies of the Lakota with his counts of coup and feats of bravery.

But when the end had come, and the people were being sent to different reservations, it was discovered Matt was a white child, and he was taken away and sent to St. Louis to a mission school where he would learn English and the ways of white. It didn't take Matt long to adapt to these ways and then make his escape and survive on his own.

The council stood and cheered as Matt arrived the council fire. Buffalo Robes began by lighting the pipe to smoke first, then talk. Each of the council members looked to one another for the one to start the council.

Buffalo Robes began, "It is good you join us once again, my son, but I must ask the reason for this visit?"

All eyes were on Matt as he began, "My father and those of the council. It is with sadness I come before you. The Army sent for me to look for you and bring the soldiers so they can return you to the reservations. But this I will not do. I come here to ask you to go back on your own because no good can come of this. Already there has been bloodshed and lives taken. There must not be a fight. The whites are too many, not like in the past. Many have come since the Lakota were taken from this land. I fear for the safety of all the people. If you tell me what angers you, I can go back to the Soldiers and tell them."

There was much mumbling, and Matt could see his speech didn't change anything. Black Elk was the first to speak. "You honor our council fire once more Pahaska, you ask what angers us to leave that place. To this I say look to the old ones, see the small ones who go hungry and get the white man's disease and die. See for yourself the young maidens who have been taken by the white soldiers. They take our young ones and teach the white way like they did to you so many moons ago. To teach that the way of the white is right, and the way of the

Lakota is wrong. This is my answer to you Pahaska."

Again, there was mumbling amongst the council, then Spotted Eagle spoke, "You ask what angers me? I say to you, look to the young men. They do not know how to be a man. They do not hunt. They do not provide for their lodge. They heard stories of your great feats when you were among us and those of Sitting Bull and Crazy Horse. They know not of the hunt for the Tatanka, and soon I fear they will know not of our tongue. This is what angers me."

Buffalo Robes begins to speak, "As chief of the Lakota, it saddens me to see and hear the pain of my people. It angers me to remember the day Crazy Horse brought the people to the White Soldier peace table to make the mark on the paper. It angers me to see our young take of the evil fire water. It brings much trouble. We stand and wait for food to fill our stomachs, and it doesn't come. When the cold winds come, we do not have robes to keep warm. As Chief of the Lakota, I do not want war with the white man. Only to live as we have lived before. To hunt and to teach our ways to our young,

There was a long silence, then Matt spoke. "To hear of the suffering of my people saddens my heart. I was aware there were many things wrong at the reservations, but not how bad it really was. It angers me that the whites would go against their word. I say to you, I will speak with the General in charge and see to it that their promises are kept. But I ask you to start heading back to the reservation. This way the Soldiers will know you don't want war."

More mumbling amongst the council, then Matt was asked to leave while they talked.

It didn't take long for him to get his answer. They had decided not to return, but he had convinced the council to not fight unless pushed into it. He knew the situation could only get worse if the fighting continued. The way the tribe was heading would take them into the area of Buffalo Flats, and Matt needed to know there would be no fighting. He thought if he could keep all parties involved separated, then the situation would most certainly get better.

Chapter Eleven

The Cavalry troop that Matt had saved from certain death now had all the wounded patched up and had buried the dead in makeshift graves. They were now on the move, and the Lieutenant was happy to see another patrol approaching from the South. He waited eagerly for the troop to link up.

The Lieutenant saluted, and the Captain ordered him to report. "Sir, yesterday we were engaged in a fight with the Sioux, and this white man riding a painted Roan rode up to the high ground and started raising his arms and signaling to the Sioux. They acted like they were happy to see him and broke off the fight and rode off with him. You don't think he was leading them to do you, Sir?"

The Captain wondered, looked this young shavetail over, thinking to himself, *how did he lead this troop and survive.*

"You really have no idea who that was, do you?" He wondered how this young soldier had survived this long. "That, Lieutenant, was the one and only Matt Hutchins, and no, he didn't lead them to fight. But, he sure saved this troop from annihilation."

The Captain surveyed the ragtag survivors and said, "You need to get these men back so the medical officer can help them. Also, report to the Major. Inform him that we have linked up with Hutchins and we're following them. Also, give him our location and that we're traveling north."

Clem was very excited to see the sheriff as he pulled up in front of the livery stable. "Bank foreclosed on the Twisted T yesterday," said Clem even before the sheriff dismounted. "Bank's waiting for you to serve the papers. There were a couple of hard cases showed up the other day. They're in the saloon wearing their holsters slung low. Looks like they know how to use them too."

"Clem you got any good news?" fussed the sheriff because he was bone tired from all the riding. "Give my horse a good going over and feed her while I go get me a bath, a shave and something to eat?"

The mayor, looking out the windows of his office, caught sight of the sheriff going to the hotel and decided he needed to talk to him, and now.

He caught him just as he was entering the hotel. "Sheriff. Glad to see you're back safe and sound. Did you have any luck with those rustlers and where is that stranger? The whole town's been talking. The council is worried about those Indians and those two strangers. They look mean Sheriff. Real mean. Women folk are starting to feel they're not safe anymore."

"Mayor, I don't want to seem rude, but right now I need a hot meal, something I ain't had in two weeks. I need time to think, and by the way, that stranger you're asking about was none other than Matt Hutchins, Chief Army Scout. He took off after those injuns. I imagine he's found them by now. Also, who told the town about the Indians being off the reservation? I thought we were gonna keep it between you and me."

"Sally! Over here!" He hollered at the waitress, then turned back to face the mayor.

"Hello Sheriff, Mr. Mayor. We've got a great meal for lunch today. Then for desert we have freshly made pie, so what's it going to be?"

"I'll have the special," the sheriff told her, "and a big slice of that pie. And please, I need coffee and plenty of it."

The mayor asked for a glass of water.

"Let me eat first Mayor," the sheriff told him. "Then we'll discuss business. That okay with you?"

The mayor, deep in thought only nodded. The sheriff figured he had something severe to talk over.

With a good meal under his belt and feeling really refreshed from his bath, the sheriff decided to go to the saloon and check out the two hard cases everybody was worried about. On the way out he asks, "Sally, is little Pete around? If he is, ask him to run down to the livery for me and tell Clem to meet me in my office."

The sheriff then headed out to the street and runs into the mayor. Holding his hand up, he tells him, "Got some business to tend to right now. Oh! The town is going to owe Clem deputy pay or at the very least jailers pay, maybe both."

The mayor knew from seeing the sheriff's face not to ask any questions. Sheriff Fry was going to do what he did best. From the look on his face, one could see he was determined. It was the hardness in his eyes and no display of emotion that he had when he was ready to take care of business.

When little Pete gave Clem the word that the sheriff wanted to see him in his office, he told Little Pete to watch the livery stable while he was gone. Halfway out the door, he turns and asks Little Pete if he knew what the sheriff wanted him for.

"All I know," said Little Pete, "is Miss Sally told me to tell you the sheriff wanted you."

As he hurried down the street, Clem thought aloud, "This must be something serious for the sheriff to send Little Pete. He usually comes to the stable himself."

As he hurries through the office door, the sheriff tells him, "Clem, get that scatter gun and give me the sawed off, load both of them. You enter the saloon from the back and be quiet about it. Stay in the shadows until you hear me brace'em, then show yourself with that scatter gun. You got that?"

Clem nodded that he understood and with the scatter gun, he headed out the door.

The sheriff made his way to the front door of the saloon, then stopped, giving Clem time to reach the back door. When he figured Clem had enough time to get there, he stepped through the front door.

"Well now," exclaimed the sheriff, "ain't this a welcoming sight to see. Charlie Logan and who's the sidewinder with you?"

The men turned to the sound of the voice, and a smile breaks on the face of the one named Logan.

"Imagine this! If it ain't Sheriff Fry. In the flesh. Long time no see Sheriff. You must be expecting trouble standing there holding that sawed off'?"

He had the shotgun level and pointed at the two men. He knew from experience this wasn't going to end well.

"Hi Charlie, staying long? If you are, you need to surrender your weapons. Now, real slow like, put them on the bar, then back away."

Logan says to his partner, "You hear that Frank, he wants us to surrender our guns. Suppose we don't want to, then what, Sheriff? Guess we could tell you the same thing? You put down that shotgun and back away."

Chairs started shuffling as men started moving fast to get out of the way. Clem entered unseen and stood there waiting for the sheriff's cue.

"Who hired you, Charlie," Fry asked, "Who you gunning for? Soon as I heard you were in town,

I got that feeling it might be me you're looking for. You ain't sore, are you Charlie, about spending, how long was it, in prison? You couldn't come by yourself, could you because you're yellow? You need a back shooter. You meet your friend in jail Charlie?"

Fry looks at Logan's partner, "Frank, is it? You fast boy? You better be real fast, because if the both of you don't put your weapons on the bar, in the time, it takes my deputy to click the chamber shut on that scatter gun he's got; you're going to be meeting your maker very shortly. Now, what's it going to be, Charlie, Frank? Well? What's the matter Frank, you're sweating? Not so sure, huh. If I were you, I wouldn't count on ole Charlie too much. He's hitting the floor in about two seconds. Clem there, is gonna get you, Frank."

The tension was so thick you could cut it with a knife. With the click of the chamber closing, it was over in the blink of an eye.

Charlie and Frank took the shotgun blasts at short range, and there was almost nothing left of them. When the smoke cleared the sheriff and Clem, as well as the onlookers, stood in disbelief that the two gunnies would go for their guns with both shotguns pointed at them. The blasts also damaged the bar and a few tables and chairs.

The sheriff looked around and asked if anybody was hit.

"Everybody's okay," someone said.

"Sure nobody was hit," Fry asked again.

The mayor appeared and demanded to know what was going on. The saloon owner wasn't very happy. "Who's gonna pay for all this damage? It'll take a month of Sundays to get the blood off the floor."

"Ask the mayor," Fry shot back, "My question is, who hired these two? Somebody has got to know something." He was certain it was someone in town and that someone was hiding something. "I've already killed two of the rustlers, and I have the head of one of them at the undertakers. I'm asking for help in identifying it."

The shootout was the talk of the town for weeks to come. Sheriff Fry had taken down Charlie Logan and Frank Deans. Peace and quiet returned to Buffalo Flats, and the word was out that this was a town that had a sheriff who meant business. Still, the question remained, who hired those two. No one seemed to know. The sheriff served the papers on the Twisted T, and it became apparent to him that the bank was getting tight with the ranchers.

The bank president was spending more and more time away from Buffalo Flats. After a while, more cattle began to turn up missing. The mayor and the town council, as usual, was up in arms over it. The town council along with the mayor had their discussions and decided they needed more peace in Buffalo Flats.

The railroad was talking with the bank president and was working on a deal to run a spur through the town. This would mean more business for the town and more people would settle there. Fry began to realize why the bank president was going out of town so much and why the bank was getting so desperate on loan payments and mortgages.

As Sheriff Fry stood before the town council, he looked at the mayor, "So how long have you been keeping this a secret?" He was referring to the railroad coming to town.

"The council and I decided to tell the people when it was a done deal."

"Any of you got any idea who might have the money to hire a gunslinger like Charlie Logan?" He looked at the five members of the council. "He didn't come cheap."

"Why would we know something like that Sheriff?" Exclaimed the mayor.

"Hold on there a minute," the sheriff stopped him. "Just where do they plan to run this spur?"

"It will come north out of Denver and link up in the north and tie into the Union Pacific at

Chicago. This town can grow, and the ranchers can move their cattle easier and faster. The farmers will be able to move their harvest to market cheaper and faster, but this won't happen unless peace with the Indians happens, making this a place to want to live in. It's also important that you catch these rustlers."

"I'll ask you again," the sheriff looked directly at him. "Why have you and the council been keeping this a secret for so long and not telling anyone? Don't you think the people would like to know and have something good to look forward to?"

The council members looked at one another and shrugged. But Stan, the banker, had other ideas. He was adamant that before they released the news, the plan should be fully completed. "As you know the bank has me serving papers of foreclosure on a lot of the ranchers and farms in the area."

"And don't you think the people will think that's a little fishy that you kept quiet about the railroad?" commented the sheriff.

The council members started squirming in their seats looking at one another. The mayor now rubbing his chin says, "Now that you brought it up it does seem fishy, but this is Stan. For heaven's sake, he wouldn't do anything like that!"

Fry gives the mayor a harsh look. "Mayor, for someone who professes to be smart at business, you're dumb at judging people. Business is a business. In business, you make money, and if there is one thing I know is that Stan is in love with money. I think he'd put his own grandmother out on the street if it meant he'd make a buck."

Chapter Twelve

"Major, this telegram just arrived," the Sergeant Major announces entering his Major's office.'

"Well hand it over, Sergeant Major and let me have a look at it. He read the words and shouted, "It seems that General Thompson and the whole regiment is coming by train. We're to take our brigade and head west, just east of Buffalo Flats, then swing north. Captain Nelson met up with your Matt Hutchins, and he's run off his scouts. It also states Hutchins saved a whole troop from being wiped out when he led the war party away from the fight. What do you think that's all about Sergeant? You know this Hutchins better than anyone else. I'm in the dark about the man."

The Sergeant walks over to the map, "Sir, if the General takes the train North from Fort Kearney and we move west, then north, we're gonna have them between the people and us in Buffalo Flats. I think Matt led those Braves away to stop the fighting and also pinpoint the hostiles and talk some sense into them. He could be with them at this very moment, but if those Indians hit those mountains before we do, with winter on the way, we're gonna have a hard time getting them out of there. I know that country. It's hilly and rocky with plenty of game. I think that's where the General is going to try to block them."

Matt rejoined the Captain and the patrol. "Good to see you again, Hutchins. That was some act of bravery getting those warriors away from that fight and saving all those men."

"Right now Captain, you're in danger. The whole Lakota people are due north of you. I convinced them to agree to no more fighting if you do the same, but I need you to hold here, wait for me to return. There's a town further north called Buffalo Flats, and they're in the path of all this. I've got to warn them and get them to let the Indians pass. There will be no fighting."

Agreeing with Matt, the Captain said, "In that case, I'll send a rider to inform the Major about this."

As soon as the Major receives the message, he orders, "Bugler, sound Officers call."

With all the officers in assembly, the Major informs them of the latest news. He then turns and asks the Sergeant Major, "What's your opinion of this agreement. Can the Sioux be trusted or will they fight."

"Major, I figure if Matt Hutchins got them to agree, then yes, we can believe this arrangement."

Matt rode 'Ole Friend hard, and Friend put a lot of real estate between them and Captain Nelson's patrol. He arrived early the next morning and headed straight to the sheriff's office.

"I never thought I'd see you again, Matt," said the sheriff as he offered his hand in greeting. "What are you doing back here?"

"This town is in the path of the Lakota," he said seriously. "They're heading right for you. I've convinced them to pass by without a fight, but they believe the buffalo are still here. They're hungry, tired, and the elderly are in sad shape. I can't believe I was the one that talked them into signing that peace treaty, only to be starved half to death."

"Come on, Matt, the mayor, needs to hear about this.

They rushed into the mayor's office. "Mayor, Matt's got something to tell you. I would advise you to listen very carefully. Go ahead, Matt."

"The Sioux are heading this way, and the town is right in their path. They think that the buffalo are still here. They've dreamed of nothing else than hunting the buffalo, and the young braves are spoiling to make a name for themselves to impress the tribal council. It wouldn't take much for this whole mess to blow up with blood being spilled on both sides."

"Mayor," exclaimed Sheriff Fry, "We've got to inform everyone to let those Indians pass by without any trouble."

As all three of them run from the office, the mayor tells Fry, "Sound the church bell and get everyone into town as soon as possible."

"Mr. Hutchins," asked the mayor, "Will they pass on by and not cause trouble? I wish I had total faith in this arrangement. I think you might be better at explaining the situation to them."

It took almost an hour for everyone from the surrounding areas to arrive. In the meantime, Matt went to the café to get some of that excellent cooking.

"Hello Mr. Hutchins," Sally said with a big smile on her face, "I was under the impression I wouldn't see you again with you being a person that doesn't like towns. It must have been something pretty important to bring you back here."

She was hoping that maybe he came back to see her. She had thought about nothing else when he left, and she felt she should have told him how she felt. However, that wasn't lady like, so she had let him ride out. But not this time. This time, she was going to tell him how she felt.

"Sally," he said, "you're a mighty fine cook, and my stomach reminded me of it ever since I left. That plus I have to let the people know about the Sioux and ask them to let them pass through without any trouble."

"Do you really think that they would pass by without any shooting or killing? And what about this town and its people, are they going to let them pass by?"

"I just met with the sheriff and the mayor. We're going to meet with the people in a bit and ask them to do just that," he explained.

The little town all of a sudden wasn't so quiet, rustlers, gunslingers gunning for the sheriff and now Indians. The sheriff laughed to himself.

"You know Matt," he said, "I've got a suspicion about the rustlers that I haven't told you about. Somebody hired a couple of gunslingers to gun me down, and the town council has been working with the bank president on getting the railroad to run a spur through here. Funny thing about all this is the bank holds the notes on all the property that the spur would cross. Maybe I'm wrong, but something smells to high heaven. Bank's having me serve foreclosure notices on the ranches that have had cattle rustled. And even on some of the little homesteads. I'm telling you I think I wasted a whole lot of time riding around out there. I should have stayed in town and began the search right here."

"You could be right, but at the time how could you have known. I thought it over because I was looking for the Sioux. The rustlers used unshod horses to cover their trail. Metal shoes would have left marks on the rocks, easy to track, but those cows are somewhere in the area even though we found no sign."

People in wagons and on horseback were coming into town. It was time for the meeting to begin. Everyone had assembled at the church as always.

The mayor called the meeting to order. "Ladies and gentlemen, please, please, Quiet please, shut up so that we can get down to business. We called you all here today to inform you about a little problem that some of you may already be aware of. The fact is that the Lakota Sioux have jumped the reservations and are in fact in our area."

This announcement caused some unsettling of the people. "Please! Please! Everyone, please settle down. We have someone with us today who's an Army Scout. Some of you may have heard about Mr. Matt Hutchins. He'll tell you everything you need to know so, please listen to what he has to say. Mr. Hutchins, if you please."

"My name is Matt Hutchins, Chief Army Scout. I'm here today to set your minds at ease about the Lakota. They have no intentions of going to war or getting into any fights. They've left the reservation because they're hungry. Most of the treaty agreements haven't been kept by the Indian Affairs Department in Washington. Believe me, when I tell you they are in no condition for a fight. They're only interested in living their lives as they always have, as a free people left to their own customs. I sat in council with them only last night, and they agreed to pass by the town without any trouble. I'm here to get the same agreement from you. Should you encounter the Lakota, you need to let them pass. If you do that, there will be no trouble."

The majority of the town people and most of the farmers were in agreement to let the Indians pass without any fighting. Of course, there's always a few who either don't agree, or they just hate Indians. One person was Justin Bourg, a cattle rancher, who has the meanest reputation of anyone in the county.

"How'd I know these so called hungry Injins ain't gonna help themselves to some of my beeves, Mr. Army Scout?" he asked loudly, "They come near my range, I'm gonna shoot first then, ask questions later, by golly."

"Now hold on there, Bourg," the sheriff said to him, "You go shooting at one of those people, I'll lock you up. Maybe I should lock you up now to simmer you down. If Matt here says they'll be no trouble, I believe him, and you best take heed. Do what he's told you and remember what I said."

"If these Indians just pass through and don't cause no trouble, then I'll protect them the same way the law protects you. Now, I want all of you to listen and hear what I say. Matt says they'll be no trouble from the Indians, and there won't be no trouble from any of us. Anybody starts something with the Indians, and I'll lock you up and throw away the key. You remember that."

The crowd started breaking up, so the mayor stood up and shouted, "Hey! Hey! Listen to me. I want to give you some good news. The reason it's so important, is the town council, along with the bank, is in talks with the railroad to bring a spur through our town. A spur like this will bring more people into the community, meaning more business and making it easier for you cattlemen to get your beef to market. And you farmers will be able to ship your harvest to market much faster. So, as you can see, we can't afford any trouble right now. Please, just let them pass."

"What about all this rustling going on, ain't that trouble?" Justin Bourg shouted. Maybe these Indians might be the ones doing the rustling."

"I've heard about enough out of you, Bourg," said the sheriff. "I'm not a man to go about repeating myself, but I'm gonna tell you one last time. You will let those people through, and you will stop trying to incite a riot. By golly, I should lock you up right now for disturbing the peace. For your information, I got two of those rustlers, and they were as white as you and the rest of us. In fact, the undertaker has a head you might take a look at to see if you can identify it if anybody has a notion of doing so."

"What happened to the rest of the poor soul?" the minister wanted to know.

"We left those two Jaspers where they dropped and seeing as how we were three days out, by the time we'd got them back, they'd have been mighty ripe if you understand me. Those two tried to dry gulch Matt and me. Darn near got us too. If anybody cares to take a look-see, be my guest."

The sheriff waited a bit for a response and getting none the meeting broke up, with everyone going their separate ways. Folks were talking about the railroad coming through and the rustlers but seemed to have forgotten about the Sioux.

Matt had made it a point to make sure everyone understood and was satisfied.

"I reckon I better get on my way and find those troopers and try to talk some sense into them. There's a bunch young soldiers just spoiling for a fight."

"But Matt?" Miss Sally asked, "Aren't you going to have something to eat before you leave?"

The sheriff could see the hope in Sally's eyes and looks at Matt "What's wrong with you Hutchins," the sheriff asked. "You can't leave without having' some of Miss Sally's excellent cooking. You should be ashamed of yourself, I would think, I bet she made something real special today just for you. Am I right, Miss Sally?"

"You're right Sheriff," she said quickly, "We got roast beef, gravy, potatoes with green beans and fresh apple pie. Also, got some freshly made bread. Made it myself just before I come over here."

"By golly, that sounds good," the mayor joins in. "If you don't mind, I think I'll have some of that." with that he said goodbye.

"Better think fast, Matt," the sheriff tells him. "Once the mayor gets there, there might be none left for you. Why just the mention of food sets him off."

"Never knew somebody that big could move so fast. Miss Sally, I think if we stay here too long, that their mayor just might eat you out of business, not to mention him leaving me any of that pie. Here I was thinking how useless the mayor is, but I reckon he is good for something. Eating!" Sally and the sheriff laughed and started towards the café with Matt following close behind.

John D. Fie Jr

Chapter Thirteen

The Indian scouting parties had been sent out in all directions and brought back the news of the Calvary patrols to the North and South, but none to the northwest.

The Chiefs decided to turn their people to the northwest. This seemed to be a better way of going because it would get them off the plains faster and into the Mountains where there was plenty of water and game. They could also avoid the Whites to the North. It took them out of their way but provided more cover. The Chiefs didn't know, but this spoiled the Army's plans of blocking them in. This, also meant that the agreements Matt had made for no fighting, was now no good, should they encounter any problems going in this new direction.

General Thompson disembarked the trains with the regiment in Cheyenne, in Wyoming territory. He then proceeded north, while the other Calvary units were outside Casper to the Northwest.

The Sioux had covered more ground faster than the Calvary had expected. The tribe was already way north of them, and now they had swung to the northwest and would surely give the Calvary the slip again. Captain Nelson grew impatient and made the decision to move his troop north against what Matt had told him. However, by the time he got to the spot where Matt had reported where the Sioux were, they were no longer there.

Black Elk had scouting parties out, and the troop and one of those scouting parties ran into one another. The Sioux thinking there would be no fighting held back while the Calvary went into a full charge and almost wiped out the entire scouting party. Only a few survived.

The few that survived reported back to the Chiefs explaining what had happened. There would be no more talk of peace. Two bands were sent now to disrupt the Calvary pursuit and give the Indians a head start. Once they were far enough away and safe from danger, the rest would join them and give the soldiers the battle that they seemed to be wanting.

Black Elk would lead both bands because of his experience and knowledge of how the Calvary fought. Up until now, there had only been minor fights, but Black Elk meant to put the fear of the Sioux into the Calvary.

He knew how to lead, and he was a proven War Chief. He was known for not taking risks, knowing when to engage and when to disengage should the advantage turn against him. He had learned many tricks from their greatest allies, the Northern Cheyenne. The Cheyenne were thought to be to the best light Calvary in the world, taking and using the Plains to their advantage in a fight.

Black Elk sent out scouting parties trying to learn where and how to attack the soldiers. They would bring the fear first to the weakest, then wait for the stronger to reinforce. Then hit them before they knew what was happening.

Once the scouting parties returned with the news, Black Elk made his plans. There was a supply train of wagons heading west, and a large body of soldiers were off to the east. Black Elk took his party to see the area, then made his final plans. He would split the war party and hit the supply train from both sides. On his signal, one of the parties would attack the rear of the supply train.

Taken by surprise, the Major had no recourse, but to move the outriders to reinforce the back of the train and that's when all hell broke out. Black Elk, seeing the front of the column was left unguarded threw the rest of the war party at the front of the train.

The Sioux swarmed over the soldiers, inflicting immediate damage to both men and wagons. It seemed like seconds, and the whole front of the train was afire with powder exploding the Sioux and soldiers in bloody hand to hand combat.

The Major confused and outnumbered broke off with what wagons he had left trying to circle them in hopes of getting what was left out of danger. Turning to Sergeant O'Reilly, he had a look of confusion and a silent plea for help.

O'Reilley taking the hint, formed what troopers that were left into skirmishers and directed fire in rapid response.

Black Elk sat astride his horse on a small knoll out of the line of fire, where he could see the soldiers to the rear were beginning to get organized, so he directed more braves to attack the rear. Soon it was over. Black Elk wanted to leave some alive to tell the story, so he called back the warriors.

The Major in shock looked around at the carnage. "Sergeant Major, did you see that devil up there on that knoll? He just sat there and directed the whole battle from start to finish."

"Aye, that I did, Sir, it was none other than Black Elk himself, Sir." The Sergeant turns and issues orders to the troop leaders to gather names of those killed and wounded and the damage to the wagon train.

"My career is ruined Sergeant, look at all this damage. They just appeared with no warning."

"Aye, Sir. They will do that. Black Elk is a tricky one, Sir. With Buffalo Robes, the two make a formidable enemy. It won't be easy taking them down. We better do it soon, before the winter sets in. It can git mighty cold out here on the plains."

"See to the wounded Sergeant and get a burial detail working. See what we can salvage out of this carnage.

The surgeons were busy at work when the lead scouting party came upon the column. "We saw your smoke Major, what a fight this must have been. The General isn't going to like this Major. I'll have to report this right away. Lieutenant, send a dispatch rider to the front."

"Yes sir, right away." Then turned to issue the order to the rider.

"Take this dispatch back to the General and make it fast." Four troopers took off with the news of the fight.

Once they reached the regiments with the report, one thousand soldiers were sent to relieve the severely beaten column. The smoke from the fires could be seen for miles, but it wasn't until three days later that Matt spotted the smoke. He quickly made his way there. The entire Calvary that was joining up there brought the column to well over 4,000 soldiers.

Matt noticed the heavy artillery and the new Gatling guns immediately. These were going to be used to destroy or at least bring the Sioux to their knees. The General was an old Indian fighter and was well aware of the Sioux tactics and how they waged war.

John D. Fie Jr

Chapter Fourteen

The entire Lakota tribe was now heading south after getting the women and children along with the elderly safely into the mountains. Stories of what Black Elk had done and his great victory had all the young braves ready and eager to join in the battle and defeat the whites who stole Sioux lands, killed off the buffalo and starved them while on those reservations. Years of suffering were now going to be avenged. Over half of the Lakota was made up of young Braves mixed with the survivors of all the fights with the whites. The older, wiser warriors were told to control the young and handle the fighting only when the conditions were in their favor. This was going to be a win or end it all fight.

The Lakota picked the ground for battle and now held the high ground with easy access to water and hidden storm washes. This place was to be used to hit the Army from all sides without being seen. The Lakota divided up the warriors to use bow and arrows while others would attack on horseback. Still, others were to use the storm washes and travel on foot to move around and cause confusion to the troops. The only thing for them to do was wait for the Army to arrive.

In the meantime, Matt was telling the General about trying to engage the Sioux on their old grounds. It had been years since they had been there, but landscape doesn't change all that much with time. The terrain in which the Sioux had chosen was filled with open plains and many storm washes which were hard to see from a distance. With mountains to the rear in which to hide made it the perfect ground for a fight.

Matt was determined to convince the General it was an unfortunate decision to engage the Sioux here. However, the General wouldn't listen. He had other plans. He had a full division of infantry dispatched and under orders to be well armed with the new repeating rifles that were packed and hidden away inside the supply trains following the main Calvary columns. Should the supply trains get hit, the infantry that was concealed in the wagons would be able to lay down a field of fire never before seen in any fight. A lot of the infantry were battle hardened from years of fighting, and they knew they had to lay down the devastating fire.

Indians on horseback were sitting ducks, should they attack. Every other wagon held a Gatling gun and repeating rifles. The general thought they were ready for battle.

Sioux scouts reported about the many soldiers and the wagons. Minds were made up quickly, two bands were sent out to get the supply trains and cut them off. Another group was assigned to draw out the enemy from the front. The rest of the Lakota began sending smoke signals with full knowledge that they could be seen by the Army.

With the war ceremonies well on the way, the war dancing began, the battle ponies were being prepared for war. It was just a matter of time.

The next morning Matt stood looking out across the plains and seeing the smoke signals. He knew he couldn't watch what was going to take place. There would be blood on the plains this day, on both sides.

Joining Matt, Captain Nelson and the Sargent Major asked Matt what the smoke was saying. Matt looked at them and told them he couldn't stay and watch the bloodbath.

"You know they are not going to hit the front of this line in a full frontal charge, don't you?" He asked them.

"Yes, experience and history tell me they'll wear us down first," replied the Captain.

As Matt looked toward the mountains, he muttered, "The General's a fool and won't listen to me. By the time they get finished with these green troops, you'll be using healthy men to tend the wounded, that's when they'll strike and strike hard. When you're the weakest." He kicked the dirt and looked again at the Captain. "I can't watch this. I can't be a part of this. You see what I'm up against, can't you?"

"Yes, Matt," replied the Captain, "And I don't blame you one bit, but for what it's worth, you tried your best to avoid this, but I guess the chess board was all set up for it to go until the end. As you said, they'll be blood on the plains today."

"Well, Captain, you take care of yourself and O'Reilley. Keep an eye out for the good Captain here. And you keep your head down too."

"Aye, Matt, me boy," said O'Reilley. "We'll be seeing one another again. You take care of yourself and stay out of trouble."

As they shook hands and said their goodbyes, guns began to roar from the rear of the encampment, loud explosions made the earth shake.

"It's started, Matt," said O'Reilley, "That sounds like it's coming from the supply trains."

"Supply trains don't move with cannons, and this was Artillery fire." He said to no one in particular. The encampment came to live as troopers began dashing everywhere as more gunfire broke out. Matt, the Captain, and O'Reilley took off running toward the headquarters tent. They got there just in time to hear the General order the guns to open upon the Sioux that was trying to draw the Army out.

"Watch this, Mr. Hutchins," the General bragged. "I, too, have fought the Sioux."

When the big guns located the Indians, it didn't take long for the Sioux to be cut to pieces by artillery fire. Some of the Sioux got a bit closer to coming up one of the storm washes. They began to fire with repeating rifles. It was only a matter of seconds, and the ground was covered with dead and dying Sioux, along with horses. It was a site like Matt had never witnessed and he knew then the fight had been a slaughter.

"Now that this little skirmish is over," the General said to Matt. "If you'll follow me, Mr. Hutchins, I have something to show you." as they entered the tent.

On a long table in the middle of the tent was a map with little figures placed on it. "Look at this, Mr. Hutchins. Wasn't it you that advised me not to engage the enemy here? These maps were made by the Army Corp. of Engineers several years ago showing the entire lay of the terrain. All the Gullies, the storm washes, and the height of the land and also the height of the mountains to the rear of the enemy, where they think they will hiding from us. But as you can see by the figures on the map, all my troops are all placed in strategic locations. Making it impossible for them to flank us or get us in a crossfire. All I have to do is sit and wait for them to come to me. Now I'll give you one last chance to talk to them. Try to talk sense into them. Remember, I've got them where I want them, Mr. Hutchins. We will chew them up and spit them out in a matter of hours, down to every last man, woman, and child. No, don't try to reason with me. Your job is out there with them. Go quickly and bring their answer directly to me."

Matt knew this trip was a waste of time, but he would make an effort anyway, even though Buffalo Robes had already said the talk of peace was over. If there were no peace without slavery, then they would all fight to the death.

Carrying a flag of truce, Matt covered ground quickly, and it wasn't long before he was picked up by forwarding Scouts of the Sioux and brought to the main camp.

Once Matt was gone the General assembled his officers for a meeting and had a little war council of his own. "Gentlemen, I have you gathered here to give you your orders. If you look at the map, you'll find your positions for the upcoming engagement. Colonel Medley, you will take a Corps of Calvary and hold them in reserve, making sure to watch my position for the signalman to send out the orders. Major Crawford, since you have already met the enemy, you will fight afoot with the infantry on the forward battlefield. You will take two battalions of infantry, two squadrons of field guns and build your earthworks after nightfall here in this storm wash. Take a good look at the map. There is only one possible point that may be vulnerable. You cover that spot with three rifle squads and a Gatling gun. All the other field gun squadrons will wait until after dark to disassemble your weapons and mount them on mules to move into position here," he pointed to a spot on the map. "Captain Nelson with one battalion of infantry will help set up the cover fire for our Calvary units once I deploy them. Captain Franks, you will do the same as Captain Nelson except you will maintain this position," pointing again to the map. "You will also back up the Calvary units. Now, Major Greeley, I understand during the great fight of civil unrest you distinguished yourself as one of General Sherman's artillery officers by laying siege to Atlanta. You, Sir, will protect the front with the rest of the field pieces. Once we open fire, I want the rapid fire of air bursts and concussion at 5,000 yards, then drop the next load at 500 yards at a time, until the enemy or what's left of them are within 1,000 meters, then change to grapeshot. Whatever is left of them after that, the Calvary will take over. Again, Major Crawford, you will open fire at 500 yards with grapeshot, and I want your guns to set up the interlocking fire to cover the whole battlefield. Don't disappoint me this time, Major. Alright Gentlemen, Are there any questions?"

With no questions, the officers stood studying the battle map.

Outside headquarters, Major Crawford, met up with Sergeant Major O'Reilley, "It's no wonder Sergeant O'Reilley, the General may have graduated from West Point as head of the class, but he's got thirty field guns and fifteen Gatling Guns for support, also has the infantry. He has every foot of the battlefield covered with supporting fire. This is not going to be a fight, Sergeant, it's going to be a slaughter. A whole Nation is going to cease to exist tomorrow. I pity the poor devils."

John D. Fie Jr

Chapter Fifteen

The two Chiefs had witnessed the whole affair from high on the bluffs. They watched as many of their warriors crossed over to the happy hunting grounds in such a short period of time, and they knew this was not the place to fight. The Army had changed their old way of fighting, and now the Sioux had to figure out a way to fight and win.

As Matt entered the Indian camp, he was met with grim faces by the Buffalo Robes and Black Face. Together they agreed to hear what Pahaska had to say.

Matt was greeted by Black Elk first, then by Buffalo Robes, "My Son, it is good to see you again. Come, sit with us, smoke and talk."

"Yes, my father, it is happy to see you once again. We must speak of this day and why you should not fight." He could see by the looks on the warriors' faces and the other Chiefs that they weren't as eager as they were to go up against the thunder sticks, as the Sioux called them.

"The soldiers have learned a new way to fight. They use thunder sticks and rifles that fire many times at once. Many warriors have gone to meet the Great Spirit today."

Concern was written on Buffalo Robes' face. "Yes my father, the soldiers learned how to fight this way when they fought one another in the great battle where the sun raises. They will use this knowledge tomorrow on my people. You must not fight their fight. If you will make peace once again and take our people into the mountains and hold up until the snow melts. There are white people in the town I spoke of that want to help the Sioux."

Hearing this started whispers among the Chiefs. Matt could see Black Elk had a look of disbelief, "We have heard this all before, Pahaska, but the whites speak with forked tongues. They do not live up to what is agreed."

Matt spoke calmly, "The agreements of the past were made with the Army. The people I speak of are town people, farmers, and ranchers. They don't want war. They want peace and also understand what the Sioux have been put through. They also have mothers, children, and elderly. By passing this town, go to the mountains and trust me to bring what you need. This is all I ask. This is not a good way to die. It is no honor to be cut to pieces by the thunder sticks."

Matt was asked to leave the council fire while they spoke.

Matt waited for the answer that he hoped would be good news. It wasn't long before he got his answer.

Buffalo Robes appeared, "We will not fight the soldiers fight; we will leave this place to join our people in the mountains, but we must strike a blow to the soldiers without the thunder sticks to show them they have not won."

Matt realized this news was better than an all-out war, and he knew better to not push it any further. The Sioux were an honorable people and to leave without exacting revenge would be a dishonor.

"I understand. Let it be known that I will no longer help the Army against my people, but the Army will bring the Blackfoot to scout for them, of this I am sure.

"There is much bad blood between you and them, my son. It would be wise to let your people deal with them. Now go to these people you speak of and tell them the Sioux will not make war against them. Tell them, their Chiefs are welcome at our fires. We will smoke the pipe and speak of peace with them."

Satisfied, Matt saddled up and headed back toward the Army camp to resign as Army Scout and then head for Buffalo Flats.

"Matt Hutchins is coming in General," said one of the soldiers.

"Send him straight to me when he arrives," were the General's orders.

As Matt rode into camp, there was much excitement. *You just may get the fight you're wanting, but it might not be the kind of fight you expected.* Matt thought to himself.

"By thunder Matt, you're a busy one ain't you?" Sergeant O'Reilley spoke with a booming voice.

"Hello there you old Irish reprobate, still hiding a jug somewhere?" he smiled at the sergeant.

O'Reilley smiles and points to his canteen.

"Well, let's have one then." Matt reaches for the canteen and takes a big swig. "My God, O'Reilley, where did you get this slop?" as he coughed and turned red.

O'Reilley guffawed loudly.

"Hate to break up your little reunion," Captain Nelson said as he walked up. "The General wants to see you, Matt." Matt enters the General's tent. "Well, well," the General looked intently at Matt. "How did the peace talks go, Hutchins?"

"Not well, General," replied Matt.

"OH?" Still, want to fight, do they?"

"Not really, General," Matt told him. "The cannons scared the daylights out of them. Spooked them pretty bad."

"But they're not coming in I take it, are they, Mr. Hutchins?"

"Nope, they ain't coming in, and I'm resigning my position as Chief of Scouts," Matt said. "I can't hang around and see what's gonna take place tomorrow. These people raised me, General. They're not coming in to starve to death. Maybe if the peace treaty was kept and they got all that was promised, we wouldn't be in this position. A lot of good people are gonna die tomorrow, and the people who raised me are gonna get the worst of it. I just can't watch, so I'm resigning."

"It's a shame to see you lose all you've worked for. You have a good record with the Army, but as you are well aware, I can't stop you. I'll tender your resignation with Washington with the morning dispatch."

After saying the goodbyes and wishing them the best, Matt prepares to jump on 'Ole Friend and head for Buffalo Flats. "Look me up O'Reilley, when and if you decide you've had enough of this Army life." He turned Friend and waves a final goodbye.

As he crested a small knoll, Matt stops and looks back on the quiet scene that tomorrow will be full of blood, dying and pain. "You know 'Ole Friend, it's a shame I couldn't get either side to reach some sort of agreement. I'm afraid this is going to be the last time we see some very good friends." Turning 'Ole Friend toward Buffalo Flats, he gives him a soft knee.

John D. Fie Jr

Chapter Sixteen

Indian Scouts had been watching the Army all day and reported to the Chiefs what was going on. Buffalo Robes and Black Elk decided to strike a blow after dark. The Scouts had told Buffalo Robes that Pahaska had left the Army camp and was going in the direction of the white people village.

Buffalo Robes smiled when he heard this and then signaled his Chiefs. They assembled behind the bluffs, hidden from the Army and watched their movement. Buffalo Robes and Black Elk saw a lot of activity on two rather large knolls away from the main camp. They could also see the soldiers were digging holes. This could mean they were going to put the dreaded thunder sticks on both knolls.

"We will wait for the sun to be in their eyes," explained Buffalo Robes. "We will send many warriors to these places before they can use the thunder sticks. They will send more soldiers to help these, and we will send more Warriors. We will then punish them and leave quickly for the mountains of our people."

The General was sure his plans to finish off the Sioux would work and decided that nothing else was going to happen today, so he took a small patrol to the south to look around. The Sioux scouting parties took in every movement and reported back to the Chiefs.

Buffalo Robes and Black Elk knowing that the head soldier had left with a small patrol, ordered a war party to follow and attack, only when they had the advantage. They would attack the first knoll where the soldiers were digging the holes for the thunder sticks, then when the soldiers sent reinforcements, another band would attack. If all went as planned, the soldiers would panic and become disoriented, giving them enough time to make their escape to the mountains.

Just as the sun was setting, the first shots could be heard from afar. The small patrol was attacked by the war party of braves. The signal went up to attack the small knoll. Overtaking the first knoll wasn't that hard and went just as planned. Reinforcements were on the way to rescue the men on the mound.

However, they arrived too late. The Sioux had overrun the small detachment digging, and once the reinforcements arrived, the Sioux broke off the attack, making the rescue party follow. The signal went up, and the rest of the warriors attacked the other knoll, but this time the detachment was ready.

Under orders to not fight a long drawn out battle, the Sioux broke off the attack and headed back towards the main tribe. Everything went well for the Sioux this day. There weren't many Sioux loses and the Sioux were now armed with repeating rifles taken from the dead soldiers and enough ammunition to last a while.

But things didn't go well for the war party attacking the small patrol. A lot of Braves went down fighting, but the main objective had been achieved. The General had been held back from the main fight.

Matt heard the gunfire in the distance. He stopped 'Ole Friend to listen for a while and thought, *don't hear no cannon fire, plenty of gunfire.* He remembered some of the tricks Buffalo Robes and Black Elk had used in the past and smiled,

"Friend, that sly old fox has done it again." With this, he turned Friend and headed back toward the fighting to have a look.

He was confident he would see lots of the dead Sioux. He found a wash, got off Friend and walked him into the wash. Then he skinned up the bank to take a peek. He didn't see what he was expecting. From the scene before him, it looked as though the Sioux had won the day. With just a quick look he knew that the Sioux now had some of the new repeating rifles. They would have a better chance with those weapons. And they taught the Army another lesson. All those big guns were of no use against a well-laid plan of attack.

Chapter Seventeen

Wagon loads of families were arriving in town, spreading the news about the Indians and the Army fighting to the north. The whole town, the ranchers, and farmers were a little confused about the events now taking place. They though an agreement had been made with Matt that there would be no fighting. They were to let the Indians pass through without any trouble.

The sheriff and the town council were also confused by the events, and they wanted some answers. If the Indians were north of town, then they had already passed by Buffalo Flats. Would the Army chase them back south again? If they only knew where Matt Hutchins was. Is he with the Indians or the Army?

The sheriff assured the town council that wherever Matt Hutchins was, he would keep his word of no fighting.

The next morning the man and the roan rode into town, stopping in front of the hotel. The man got down from the saddle and tied Friend's reigns to the hitching rail.

A crowd began to gather and started asking questions. Matt smiled and entered the hotel dining room. "Oh, Matt!" exclaimed Miss Sally, "I'm so happy to see you! I was anxious about you, are you alright? You're not hurt, are you?"

Matt could tell from the expression on her face that she was really concerned about his well-being. "Why, Miss Sally, why are you taking on so? Of course, I'm alright. Nothing could keep me from your good cooking."

"Does the sheriff know you're back?" she asked. "He's been worried too."

Matt wasn't used to all this concern and attention and sat thinking before he spoke. "No. I don't believe that he knows, however, with the crowd gathering outside, I'm sure he'll come bursting through the door any second."

Laughing, Sally poured a cup of coffee, "You sit right there. I'll bring you something to eat."

Clem had spotted Matt riding past the stable and made a beeline to inform the sheriff that Matt was back and over at Miss Sally's. The mayor heard the news and also headed for the hotel.

The sheriff and the mayor reached the dining room door at the same time and got stuck as they tried to get through.

Matt laughed and said, "That doorway ain't large enough for you, Sheriff, especially if you're gonna try it with the mayor at the same time."

The sheriff commented, "That's one of the reasons I like you, Matt. You're a load of laughs."

The mayor wasn't amused by their remarks, "I would think you'd have a little respect for my position as the town mayor."

"Matt," said the sheriff, "Everybody's beside themselves about the Indians and the Army, they're worried that the Army will push the Sioux back this way. How did they get north so fast after you told us they were heading this way?"

"Looks like after they had agreed to no fighting, they turned west and then north to avoid both the town and the Army. Buffalo Robes had scouting parties out and knew about the town and the whereabouts of the Army long before I got there. After what I saw yesterday with the Army, the only pushing that took place was by the Sioux. The Army didn't beat them in battle, at least not this time."

"What happened yesterday?" asked both the sheriff and the mayor.

Matt began setting the scene as he saw it and explained how Buffalo Robes and Black Elk together were a very formidable enemy

"I don't know all the details, but I resigned as Chief of Scouts and left the encampment after seeing what the General had planned for the Sioux. I could only imagine what a slaughter it was going to be and the end of the people that saved my life and raised me. I couldn't stay and watch, and the

Sioux wouldn't listen to me about another peace agreement. Not and live under the conditions they've been living under. I heard gunfire from far off, so I turned back to see what was happening. By the time I got there, it was all over. I took a quick peek from a storm wash. Buffalo Robes and Black Elk had managed to get the cannons and Gatling guns the General had set up, and I would say the Sioux won a battle yesterday. The Army took a beating, but I'm afraid the war's not over yet."

The General was in a horrible mood after seeing the damage that was done. "How could a bunch of wild savages with hardly any weapons do so much damage? Well, I guess they're properly armed now, aren't they? With our repeating rifles no less and plenty ammo. I want answers, Gentlemen, and fast."

There was no reply? The Army got caught flat footed and got beat and beat badly. No one had any answers, except Sergeant O'Reilley. "Sir; if the General would allow me to speak?"

"Certainly Sergeant Major. It seems everyone else has lost their voices."

"Well Sir," he began. "Trying to surprise Buffalo Robes and Black Elk in this country ain't gonna be easy, plus trying to fight them like we did yesterday just ain't gonna work. They'll keep hitting us and wear us down. We ain't got enough water in the water wagons now. We lost four wagons, plus munitions. The wagons we got left is gonna have to be used for the wounded. We got a little over three hundred injured and a hundred twenty-five killed. And they might hit us again tomorrow, but I have a feeling they're gonna make a run for the mountains. It'll be the devil to pay, trying to get them out of there with winter coming on. Them mountain passes are gonna be snowed in, and if we're caught up there fighting, we'll be there 'til the snow melts."

The General pacing back and forth seemed to be in deep concentration. Turning towards the Sergeant Major and the officers in attendance, he began speaking, "That's a very complete report Sergeant Major, and as usual you're right. Getting caught in those mountains without provisions would be a sure disaster. The column already has too many wounded to deal with. Looks as if we've been outfoxed once more. All we can do at this point is to make a report on the damage to Washington and wait for their answer. I've got a feeling heads are going to roll over this one."

Feeling dejected and disgusted, the General orders a complete damage report and head count on able-bodied men. "Sergeant Major, once the story is complete send a dispatch rider to the nearest telegraph office to send it to Washington."

"Sir," O'Reilley told him. "The nearest telegraph is in Buffalo Flats. Is the General sure he wants a telegram sent out over the wire describing what happened here? Or maybe just a brief report followed with a full description by dispatch courier."

"I see what you're saying, Sergeant Major. The news is bad enough, and we surely don't need it spread around the country before Washington hears about it. Yes, by all means, take care of it as you see fit."

"Excellent, Sir," O'Reilley said, "The rider will be on the way in the morning. Will that be all, Sir?"

"Yes Sergeant Major, you're dismissed, as well as all of you." Indicating the others. All the officers snapped to attention, saluted and filed out.

O'Reilley and Captain Nelson walked together on their way over to the troop area. "Captain," said O'Reilley. "I'm afraid the General is a little too worried about what happened."

Turning and looking at the General's tent, Captain Nelson made a comment, "I would be too, Sergeant. Being outfoxed by an outnumbered enemy and the damage they managed to inflict on us and the body count is horrific. Trained troops. By gosh, Headquarters will be all over this one. If he had only listened to Matt, he could have brought them in after a spell. I know it. All we had to do was wait."

"Aye Captain. Matt would surely have gotten it done and without all the bloodshed. The General wanted to make a name for himself as an Indian fighter because it would be a big boost to his career. I reckon what happened here will get the higher-ups to notice him, but not the way he wanted. I'm afraid it's going to cost him. Reminds me of what happened after Bull Run, when the Rebels gave us a spanking. Heads were served up on the silver platters."

"I missed that one Sergeant, but I heard about it. I didn't think the plans for this engagement was going to work. Even before we left, my mind was full of doubts. Those people out there have a lot of resentments in the way they've been treated, and I had a feeling it wasn't going to end well. If I were in their place, I would probably feel exactly the way they do. I learned that, after fighting the Apache in Arizona territory. Of course, Matt was a huge help and gave excellent advice, but he's not going to give advice here I'm afraid, not against the people who raised him, and we can't blame him neither."

"Aye Captain, but I don't think this is over yet. The Lakota made strong medicine today, but we're still in good enough shape to give them a fight, and they know it. We would be wise to double the guards tonight and hobble the horses. Maybe even move the horse's inside the picket line so we won't be walking back. They'll surely be up to some horse stealing and stampeding the horses."

"Good idea, Sergeant, see to it. I'll inform the General of what we're doing and why. Goodnight

Sergeant. I think I'll hit my bed roll early, just in case."

"Good night, Sir." O'Reilley issued the orders to move the horses inside the picket lines and double the guard. He wondered if they should extinguish all the camp fires to darken the encampment and make sure there was as little movement inside the picket line as possible.

It was uneventful, and as the new day was dawning, Sergeant O'Reilley was getting the dispatch rider ready for his ride to Buffalo Flats. "You're too high tail it to this town south of here and send this telegraph to the War Dept. in Washington. Ride fast and get back with their answer." The trooper was off and riding like the wind.

As the rider left the encampment, the Sioux took out after him trying to stop him. However, with all the supporting fire coming from the troops caused them to stop. "Looks like he made it Sir," came the shout from the Sergeant Major.

One of the troopers seeing this last bit of excitement was worried about being surrounded and asked the Sergeant, "Are we in trouble, Sergeant?"

"Strictly routine," O'Reilley chuckled, "We're not surrounded, but you can count on them watching us. Carry on Trooper."

His horse was lathered and winded when the dispatch rider arrived in Buffalo Flats. His arrival instantly caused a stir. The town folks, as well as the ranchers and farmers, swarmed in front of the telegraph office to see what was happening.

Clem, of course, made a beeline toward the hotel where the sheriff was eating breakfast.

After listening to Clem, he told Clem to locate Matt, then he headed for the telegraph office.

"All right, everybody, make room here, back away from the door and settle down," ordered the sheriff, "As soon as I learn something, I'll let you know. Now, go on about your business.

Clem was banging on Matt's door so hard it almost took it off the hinges. "What's so dang important you got to bust in my door?" Matt asked as he opened the door.

Clem settled down enough to tell Matt about the Army rider and the telegraph office. "I reckon if they wanted me they'd come get me, wouldn't they? But they must have sent you, am I right? Since you near broke down the door, I might get tidied up and go down for some vittles."

"Ain't you gonna go see what's going on?" Clem asked.

"Nope," replied Matt. "Eating is more important. Shut the door when you leave, will you, Clem?"

"Don't that beat all," said Clem talking to himself. When he reached the lobby, he saw the desk clerk, pointed up the stairs and pronounced, "That fella Matt sure is a strange one, never met a body like him before."

Laughing, the desk clerk had to agree,

"Yeah, that's one uncut diamond for sure. Why, when he first come in here, I could smell him coming up the street. Thought my paint was gonna peel off the walls and tarnish the brass. He even insulted the sheriff's delicate sense of smell."

"That ain't none too hard to do with the sheriff. Why I even insult it pert near every day. I have to remind him it ain't Saturday yet. That's when I take my bath that is most of the time."

The desk clerk looks at Clem then frowned, "Well Clem, Saturday or not, you do thicken the air at times."

"Now if'n you're gonna insult me, I think I'll mosey on outta here."

Clem, almost out the door, hears the desk clerk holler, "Only if you're sweet smelling!"

Clem stopped, turned and shook his fist at the Tom. "Ha, ha, ha, everyone's trying to be funny today."

John D. Fie Jr

Chapter Eighteen

The crowd, in front of the telegraph office, was excited and befuddled about Matt seemingly not being interested in the news.

"Sheriff," Clem said. "Matt ain't the least bit concerned with what's going on here. He said he was gonna git somethin' to eat. He sure is one strange fella."

"Did you wake him up, Clem?" asked the sheriff.

Clem hung his head and mumbled, "Yes, I woke him up."

"Clem, how would you like somebody waking you up with some kind of news, especially on an empty stomach?"

"Never thought about it that way. I reckon I'd be a little touchy too."

The trooper finally came out of the telegraph office and was immediately surrounded by the people asking all kinds of questions, all at once.

Sheriff Fry elbowed his way to stand by the trooper. "Now I told you, folks, to break it up. Now I'm telling you again, give this young man some room." Turning to the young trooper, "You must be tired Son. Follow me, and we'll get you cleaned up and get a hot meal in your belly. Clem, see to the trooper's mount, clean him up a bit. That is one worn out Horse."

The trooper and the sheriff walked into the cafe followed by the mayor. "Question and answer time, huh mayor?" Matt says with a smile.

"You just mind your own business," fired the mayor.

"Sit here, Trooper." The sheriff pulled out a chair for him. "Sally, we need coffee, let him be and get his belly full before you start with the questions, okay Mayor?" Besides, he can't tell you nothing 'cause that was an official Army dispatch."

Matt began to talk but was interrupted by a man running down the street shouting. Indians! Down the street!"

"What in tarnation is this all about now?" the sheriff ran to the door.

Matt was on his feet and was right behind the sheriff. They ran into the banker yelling, "Indians! Indians!"

Matt grabbed hold of him and tried to find out where the Indians were. All the man could do at this point.

Looking toward the west, Matt could see a band of braves sitting on their horses on a grassy knoll just beyond the town limits.

"Matt," asked the sheriff, "what do you suppose this is about?"

"Don't rightly know, Sheriff, but I aim to find out. You coming?"

The sheriff notices Matt doesn't have his guns. "Don't you think you need your guns?"

Matt smiles and keeps walking toward the Braves. The town folk began cheering that now they would learn something. As he reached the Indians, there was much joy and laughter as they thought it funny to see the great Pahaska without any weapons.

Sally standing in the middle of the street was worried. She had never seen anything like this in her life. But her thoughts and concerns were for Matt. Was she getting attached to this Frontiersmen? This man of the outdoors who didn't like towns and didn't like people. A man that slept on the ground and called it home. She had to laugh at herself about this concern and worry? This man, this Frontiersmen was quite able to handle anything that came his way. Yet he had assured her nothing could keep him from her cooking. Look at him, she thought, walking right up to those Indians like nothing is wrong.

"Now what in blue blazes is that fella up to now, Miss Sally?" asked Clem

"It looks to me like some Indians are here to speak to Matt," Sally answered.

Clem stood with his mouth hanging open at the sight

Laughing, Sally said, "Clem, close your mouth, you're catching flies."

"Yes ma'am," was his reply.

Sally was asking the same question, as Matt came face to face with the Indians. From what she could see, they had fun and talking. Four of them got off their horses, formed a circle, and sat down with Matt and the Sheriff.

"Great one," the brave began, "your father has sent us to get you to come to council."

Matt had hesitated before he said anything. "Does Dancing Bear know what my father wants to talk about?"

The Braves began mumbling, then one brave spoke up.

"This we do not know, Great One. We were told to seek you out to come. This is what we have been told."

"Alright," said Matt. "I'll come, but where are the people now?" he looked to Dancing Bear for the answer.

This question caused lots of confusion amongst the Braves, and finally, the solution was left to Dancing Bear.

"Dancing Bear cannot say this to you, Great One with the white eyes here to listen." The sheriff started to leave when Matt interjected. "This is the sheriff of this village that you now visit, Dancing Bear. He keeps the peace here. Do not dishonor him by not trusting him? We will eat, make talk, then you can see he is one to be trusted,"

Turning to the Sheriff Matt asked, "You think you can get someone to bring some food and water? We will counsel here and talk while we eat?"

"I'll see to it right away," the sheriff says as he begins to walk away. He signals for someone to meet him.

Clem came and met the sheriff.

"Is there something wrong Sheriff?" he asked. "What do those red devils want?"

"Never mind that Clem?" he told him, "You get Sally and help her get plenty of food and water."

"Do what you're told, Clem. Get together some food and water, and do it pronto."

"Mighty strange things going on around here today, a body can't make heads nor tails out of such goings on…. I'll tell you!" Complained Clem.

"Just get moving Clem. Stop wasting time and put your eyeballs back in your head."

Clem takes off running to Sally and tells her what is needed, and the both of them need to get it done as fast as possible.

Matt sees both Clem and Sally coming with the food and water and signals for the sheriff to help them with the food.

"I'm sorry, but we don't need any more of our kind out here with us. They are hesitant about you, Sheriff, so we don't need two more," Matt explains. "Sally, we're thankful for the food and water for the Warriors. Now please, you and Clem go back to town and tell everyone everything is okay."

"Okay Matt," Sally grabs his hand. "Good luck." She and Clem walk away.

"There is much food, my brothers," said Matt indicating the food. "Let's drink and eat and make talk." Dancing Bear was the first to speak about the big fight and the weapons and food they captured from the Army. "But," he continued, "Black Elk and Buffalo Robes worry about the winter. The people have made it into the mountains, and soon the snows will come. It will become very hard for anyone to come and go. The mountains have been a good winter place to hunt and fish in the past, but they worry about the Army. The Chiefs do not want war, but the Pony Soldiers make it hard not to fight. This is why the great one is being called."

Matt couldn't help but think back when Buffalo Robes told him there would be no peace agreement. What had changed? He wondered, is there something up his father's sleeves to try to dupe the Army? Maybe gain time in hopes the snows would fall early, and they could spend the winter in camp. Then, before the south pass opened in the spring, they could make a run for it over the summit to the north. They would gain miles and days on the Army.

"Tell my father," Matt told them. "I will come to council. I will follow in three periods of sleep."

Dancing Bear looked as if wanted to say something, but didn't and gave the signal to ride.

"I don't know what they're up to, Fry, but whatever it is, I'm bringing you along. It's Time you met my father and the rest of my people."

"Who's going to keep order here and make sure panic doesn't spread like wildfire?" was his reply.

"Simple." Matt explained, "We'll take the ones that will spread the fear with us. We'll call them peacekeepers. The Sioux call it Akicita when this was formed between the Sioux and the town. You'll be friends. Just make sure that whatever is agreed upon and promised that they will be kept. The town will never have to worry about trouble with the Sioux."

With a look of relief on his face, the sheriff started smiling. "Hey, let's bring the mayor. Make him earn his money for a change. He says we should respect his position."

Laughing they started to compile a list. Number one and two on it were the mayor and banker. "Good idea, Matt, getting the bank involved. I still have that conch we found. If I could tie him in with the rustling business, it would be over. Funny thing, though, no more rustling since the Indians showed up. And another thing, there hasn't been all those out of town business trips."

"Right," Matt said. Put down the store keeper too. He seems to be quite a gossip."

They both laughed, and the sheriff says, "I'll put Clem in charge while we're gone. It'll make him feel important. He likes to know everything that's going on."

"Anyone else you can think of?" Matt asked, looking toward the sheriff.

"Well, we do have one big mouth rancher. Says he'll take on the whole Lakota nation if they step foot on his land," added the sheriff.

"I think we better leave him behind, but have Clem keep a close eye on him or better yet, lock him up for something. That's an even better idea."

Not wanting to leave any stones unturned, Matt went into deep thought. Turning toward the sheriff, he says, "I think I'll send my own telegram to Washington. I'll give them my situation and condition report. I gave myself three days before the meeting with Buffalo Robes and Black Elk, so there should be plenty of time for an answer." Pausing, Matt looks out onto the plains and begins to think again. Then begins, "Yes, that's the answer. I tell them in my own words about what has happened and what is going to happen."

Looking a little confused the sheriff asks, "What have you got going on in that mind of yours, Matt?"

John D. Fie Jr

Chapter Nineteen

"We have a Presidential election coming up, don't we?" Without waiting for an answer, he continues. "There's a Career Military Officer in charge looking to make a name for himself. Right now the military gets anything they want with a friend in the President's chair in the White House. The last thing that the military needs are a full-blown war with the Plains Tribes and believe me, what happened out there in the last fight gave the Indians strong medicine. The other tribes like the Dakota up in the Black Hills and the Northern Cheyenne will hear about it. If the others feel that medicine is powerful enough, they'll make a break for it and join up with Buffalo Robes. Make no mistake about."

"That's all we need Matt, but do you think a telegram warning the War Dept. in your own words is gonna work?"

"I don't know, but I have to try. That's all I can do at this point. Maybe plant a seed of doubt in a few career minds and set the wheels in motion. The newspapers will most likely pick up on it, and I won't be surprised if we don't see some paper people come here. From what I hear about Washington, it's hard to keep secrets, and the newspapers are always looking and digging for stories. The Army don't like those reporters snooping around.

The General is pushing for a big fight. He's an old Indian fighter from before the big ruckus between the North and South. He wants a full pitch battle, but he's not going to get it. He brought along artillery and Gatling Guns for this. I think maybe he's forgotten how to fight Indians. They won't go charging in. They'll keep their distance and pick him apart piece by piece. They'll inflict as much damage as they can to gain the advantage and then when their medicine is unyielding, that's when the Sioux will hit him with everything they got. By this time, they'll be stronger because their friends, the Dakota and Cheyenne will be with them."

"Looks so beautiful out there, it's hard to believe that just beyond that horizon, there are two different people. One seeking to live life in their own way in their own traditions, the other pushing their will on them telling them their way is the right way." The sheriff says with feeling, "I never disagreed with putting those people on reservations, but I never saw the conditions they were forced to live under. You know Matt, I can't blame them for wanting to live their own way."

"I'm glad to see you feel this way because when we get there and sit in council, Buffalo Robes will look into your eyes. He'll watch to see if you mean it. Let's get over to the telegraph office and get that wire sent."

It didn't take long for an answer to arrive from Washington City for the General. The telegraph agent ran it over to the trooper now having a drink in the saloon. "Hey soldier boy, this here Telegraph says to rush it."

Everyone in the Saloon stopped and waited to hear if there was any information, but none was given. The only thing that was learned was that the soldier was to get on his way and not fool around.

Matt was organizing the party that would accompany them to meet Buffalo Robes and Black Elk. The mayor and banker weren't too keen on the idea of having to go along. But the way Matt and Sheriff Fry backed them into the corner they couldn't refuse. We'll hold another town meeting this evening and bring everyone up to date. Clem, you go and spread the word. We want everyone in attendance.

"Now," Matt explained to Fry. "To make a real peace maker's council, we'll need at least six to come with us, any other trouble makers you can think of?" He asked.

"None I can think of at the moment," replied the sheriff.

"Good," said Matt, "We'll take six with us. We need at least one more."

Clem had the Soldier's horse saddled and ready to ride, but the soldier was intent on finding Matt. Seeing both Matt and the sheriff walking his way, he waves to Matt to come over.

"Sir, I've got to return with this telegram, but before I go, I need to know if those Indians really want war?"

Looking at the young trooper, Matt could tell he was scared. "Son, those Indians have been mistreated terribly. They've been starved near to death and forced to do things against the treaty, and still, they don't wish for war. Not even a fight. All they want is to live in peace and raise their young with their own customs and ways, that's all. The Army is forcing these fights. If they had just left it to me, I could most likely have brought them in without any bloodshed."

Standing there shaking his head in agreement, the young trooper told Matt of what he was ordered to do while they were on the reservation and wasn't proud of it. Matt gave the soldier an understanding look, shook hands with him and said, "Good luck." The soldier mounted and was on his way.

"There goes one scared kid," Matt said to Fry. "It's a shame they're being ordered to do this while knowing that the Sioux have every right to live in peace. We've got to find a way to stop this or at least stall for time."

Fry shook his head in agreement.

The waiting game had begun now that Matt had sent the telegram to Washington. He had left orders with the telegraph office that he was to be notified as soon as an answer came in.

At the town meeting, it looked as if the whole territory was there. Matt called the meeting to order and started off by telling everyone what had been happening. "The Sioux are heading into the mountains, and I think they're hoping the snows will close the pass behind them. I've been asked to meet with them again. I don't have any idea what the meeting will be about, but I'm taking six people with me. The mayor, the banker, Charlie from the General Store, Sheriff Fry, and one other. Does any of you want to volunteer? This is a peaceful trip, and I don't think there'll be any problems."

"Why me?" Hawkins, the store owner, asked. "What do you need me for?" Both Fry and Matt couldn't hold back the smile that showed on their faces.

"Charlie," Sheriff Fry said. "You own the store, and maybe, you can do some business with these people, that's why you're going."

Matt spoke up and said, "I've sent a telegram to Washington explaining the situation with the Indians. It's my hope that they'll let me handle this and stop further bloodshed. I'm also hoping to convince Washington to let the Sioux stay in the mountains. You ranchers can then sell beef to feed the Sioux and you Charley," he nodded to the store owner, "will most likely start doing business with them. Everyone can benefit from this agreement without bloodshed," he continued. "You'll find the Sioux to be good friends once they've stopped being pushed around."

The people began mumbling and a lot of head shaking in agreement, but there were a few, as always they didn't agree. Sheriff Fry would have to keep a close watch on them.

Chapter Twenty

The soldier with the telegram for the General arrived back at the encampment.

"Rider coming in, Sir. Looks like the dispatch rider," announced the Sergeant Major. The majority of the officers had been hoping it would take longer for the return of the dispatch rider. The telegram was handed to the General, and he opened it.

"Gentlemen," he said. "It looks as though I've been relieved of command. The War Department has issued orders to retain Matt Hutchins as the new Indian Agent. He will make all attempts to settle this without any more bloodshed. We've been ordered back to our posts where I'll then turn command over to my replacement, which will be announced upon our return." Very grim-faced officers in attendance knew what this meant; the first head had rolled!

Matt read the telegram from Washington aloud, so everyone in the room was made aware that he was indeed in charge of making peace and that his plans were seriously being considered if he could get the Sioux to agree to terms. Matt and Sheriff Fry were jubilant with this message from Washington. Matt felt sure the Sioux would agree as long as he was handling the peace agreement.

"We'll leave at first light in the morning, so everyone going with us be ready," Matt announced.

Some of the men going wondered why they had to leave so early, but knew better than to question Matt. Sheriff Fry left Clem in charge of keeping order, and he made sure the mayor would pay him.

The morning came too fast for most. Clem had all the horses saddled and ready to go. Provisions were supplied by the store keeper and loaded up on a pack mule. With a lot of moaning, the reluctant companions mounted up and headed out of town for the meeting with the Indians.

A few folks waved goodbye and wished them a safe trip. Miss Sally, standing in front of the hotel had a sad look on her face. Matt could tell she was worried. He guided 'Ole Friend over and stopped.

"Miss Sally," he said to her, "you ain't got nothing to worry about. These are my people. Buffalo Robes is my father."

"Matt," she said as a tear slid down her cheek. "I can't help it. I'm very fond of you. I want you to come back."

"Please don't carry on so," he was sad when he saw her tears. "We'll talk about this when I get back in a few days. Okay?"

He tipped his hat, turned 'Ole Friend and fell in behind the others.

As he pulled up beside the sheriff, Fry said, "Notice anything different about the banker?"

"No," answered Matt. "Haven't noticed anything different. He's still shooting off his mouth, nothing unusual about that."

"Next time you get a chance, have a look see at his hat. It Looks to me like the people of this town have a swindler, thief and cattle rustler handling all their money. He seemed mighty uneasy about going with us to this meeting."

"We'll head first where the Army is camped," Matt told them. "I'll show the General the telegram and explain my plans."

"How far are they from here?" Charlie wanted to know.

"A good day and a half I'd say," Matt answered. "We'll camp in a buffalo wallow I know about a little further on, then tomorrow we'll reach their camp by noon. We'll make a cold camp tonight and move out early at daybreak."

"Mayor you alright," asked Matt. "You look all tuckered out, and how about you, Mr. Banker, you a little sore?" He was curious on how the banker was holding up. Everyone was saddle sore, and it showed, but not the banker, he was fresh as a daisy.

"You don't have to worry about me, Mr. Hutchins. I'll be just fine, soon as we eat," The mayor informed Matt.

"I wouldn't think you'd be any worse for wear with all that soft cushioning you got there," laughed Fry. "Must be a real smooth ride. I'm more worried about your poor horse."

Matt turned away, trying not to laugh, but with everyone else laughing, he had to join in. The mayor looked at the sheriff with hatred written on his face.

"You know Fry," the mayor exclaimed, "you're lucky the town elected you sheriff. If you were hired, I'd fire you for that statement."

"Enough of this tea social," Matt shouted, "Mount up and let's get moving,

The sheriff rode up beside Matt and said, "See the reaction from our banker friend? He doesn't like me because I discovered his little secret with the railroad dealings. If I could tie that in with all the land foreclosures and missing cattle, we could say goodbye to him for a long time."

Matt chuckled, "There's no doubt in my mind that he's your huckleberry alright. He's as fresh as a daisy just like he was this morning. He's been doing a lot of riding, and his hat band is missing a conch. He's been rustling cattle making it hard for the ranchers to pay the bank, then he waited until he knew the railroad was coming this way and which route it was taking, all done in top secret. Yep. He's your man alright."

"I just thought of something," the sheriff said. All those foreclosures are south of town. There're homesteads and one ranch north of town. That one ranch never had a cow go missing and no foreclosures in that direction.

Matt laughs and says, "You need to dig your spurs into that banker. There's a wound there with a scab on it, and it looks like its festering. You may want to flush that sore."

"You mean right now?"

"Sure, see if you can pick at that scab a little."

"I'll do it tonight while we're camped."

Charlie pulls up beside them and asks, "What're you two doing up here laughing and having a fun time. All they're doing is complaining."

"What are they complaining about, Charlie?" asks the sheriff.

John D. Fie Jr

Chapter Twenty One

"About you sheriff," Charlie tells him. "Matt? When we gonna make camp?"

"Sore at me, are they, Charlie?" The sheriff wants to know.

"Sore ain't the word for what they're saying. They want to find somebody else for sheriff come next election," Charlie explained.

"They just don't like that I don't knuckle under to them, and I follow the letter of the law. That's the problem."

"Fry, you stay here and watch over those two yahoos. Charlie and I are gonna scout ahead for water. The horses are gonna need water the next time we take a break. It's not far too where I plan to camp for the night, probably another five miles or so."

"That sounds good Matt," said Fry. "Meantime, I'll have a little chat with my friends."

"Come on, Charlie," Matt headed out. "Let's get moving and find water. If I remember right, we should find a storm runoff not too far ahead. With all the rain we've had. Lately, we should find plenty of water there. We'll get a better lay of the land when we hit that knobby knoll yonder," Matt pointed.

Charlie stood in the stir-ups and shielding his eyes searching the horizon. "What knoll? I can't see any hill."

"You should get out more Charlie," Matt teased him. Giving Friend a knee, he moved out with Charlie following. When they reached the knoll, they found the storm runoff had no water. They rode back over the knoll, then watched as the rest of the party headed their way.

"There they are," shouted Charlie, "I can see them, Matt."

"Yeah, I saw them a while ago, and they're sure taking their sweet time getting here. At this rate, it's gonna take, the better part of an hour to get here."

"It's getting late," Charlie said, "And you said we got five or six miles to go. It's gonna be after dark by the time we set up camp."

"You're right Charlie," said Matt. "It will be almost dark by the time we get to the place I plan to camp. But water or not we'll be staying there for the night."

The men were arguing about the law when they finally reached Matt and Charlie. Matt hollered for them to quiet down and water the animals, so they could move on and reach the spot where he planned to camp. Matt told Charlie to break out some jerky to eat.

It was a long and exhausting day and with the sun beating down on them. Both the horses and riders couldn't go much further, so Matt told them to stop. He went ahead alone, searching the area. When Friend's ears perked up and gave out a small snicker, Matt dismounted and placed his hand over Friend's nose. He then moved forward slowly and quietly. Matt could feel it in the air. Water. As he approached the depression, he could see water in the bottom of the Buffalo Wallow. He rode back and gave the all clear to the party, so they moved up and set up camp. There was plenty of dry wood from a dead tree that had been struck by lightning, so Matt decided it would be okay to have a fire. With dry wood, there wouldn't be any smoke, and the light from the campfire couldn't be seen because of the depth of the depression.

The sheriff started making the coffee as soon as the fire was going, Charlie got busy stirring up some salt pork and beans. The men were too tired and weary from the day to do much talking, and everyone hit their bedrolls soon after they had a meal.

Matt stayed awake longer. He walked over to the horses to make sure they were hobbled and had good grazing. Matt wasn't surprised to find 'Ole

Friend taking control of the other horse's and was lording over them. It made him laugh, and he said to Friend, "We're amongst a bunch of greenhorns, Friend. Even their horses are green."

He walked back to camp and settled down for the night. He didn't set up a watch because he knew 'Ole Friend was the best watch of all.

Dawn came fast with the sun rising. Matt was up first, got the fire and the coffee going. Soon the smell of fresh coffee brewing had everybody up and stirring. Charlie was first, followed by Sheriff Fry. Together they mixed up a batch of biscuits. After everyone had eaten and were saddling the horses, Charlie noticed the mayor was having trouble saddling his horse, and the banker showed him how to do it. He taps the sheriff on the arm and nods his head toward them. The sheriff smiles at Matt, and he smiles back, nodding his head.

After mounting up and moving out, the men seemed to be getting nervous. They saw nothing but trees on the first day, and a few cattle, but now there was nothing but, as Matt had called it, Buffalo Grass. They needed a rest, and Matt knew it, but he also knew they were close. Up ahead was the storm wash that Matt had peeked over and watched the end of the fight that first day. Turning, he told them, "The Army is only a little further.

When the mayor shouted, "Indians!" Matt turned quickly and said, "be quiet."

"It's just a scouting party," he explained, "keeping watch on the Army. They see me, and you're safe, so don't worry."

The scouting party began shadowing the group. Matt turned Ole Friend and told everyone, "Keep your hands off your guns and keep moving. I'll be back shortly."

He rode up to the scouting party, and they greeted him with much joy. He gave them a message to take to Buffalo Robes. He was bringing a small party with him of those that could be trusted and that he had good news.

He rejoined his party and told everyone he had sent a message to Buffalo Robes that they were on their way and would be in the camp tomorrow. Everyone from the sheriff to the banker had a look of apprehension on their faces.

Matt assured them they were safe, and there was nothing to worry about. As they rode a little further, they crested a rise and could see the Army camp.

"There's the Army camp, gentlemen. "You'll get your fill of Army chow tonight. We'll stay the night and head for the Lakota camp tomorrow. Get a good night's rest. We'll be leaving early in the morning."

"I have to admit it, but riding with you Matt, I'm getting kind of used to starting out early," The sheriff said.

"I believe in getting a good start before the sun comes up too high in the sky. By midday it starts getting a lot hotter," Matt added

"I'm an early riser myself," Charlie said." I open the store right after sun up every day, except Sunday. I go to church on Sunday."

"You'll do well tomorrow. The Lakota trust a spiritual person," Matt told him.

Chapter Twenty Two

The sentry stopped them at the edge of the camp and asked them to identify themselves. "Halt! Advance and identify yourself," he ordered.

"At ease Sentry." Matt could hear Sergeant Riley's voice as he headed their way.

"You might as well get off your horses," Matt told the men. "Walk them a bit to cool them off."

"Matthew, Matthew me boy, I'm glad to see you, greeting Matt with both arms outstretched and taps him on the shoulders.

"I see you still got your hair, you old Irish scoundrel," added Matt.

"Aye; but it was touch and go for a little bit, I'll tell you. It's the lads Matt, they got no experience and half of them wet their pants when the going gets tough."

"You know that's nothing to be ashamed of the first time out. I remember my first with the Black Foot."

"I think mine was at Shiloh or Bull Run, can't remember which. All those Rebs running and yelling. What a ruckus. Private! Come over here and take Matt's horse. Make sure he's properly cared for. I'm holding you responsible."

"Yes, Sergeant Major." The private snaps to attention salutes and off he goes with Ole Friend.

"I reckon you'll be wanting' to see the General? He's in a horrible mood since the other day when the rider got back with that telegram. He's been relieved of command, and all the officers are also in a terrible mood, they are."

As they reached the General's tent, they were met by the officer of the day. "Dismissed, Sergeant Major," he said. "This way, Sir," he motioned Matt to the tent.

"Mr. Hutchins, Sir." As Matt entered, he saw, a worried and beaten man. "There you are, Mr. Hutchins. I suppose you've heard I've been relieved of this command?"

"No, I hadn't heard. I'm mighty sorry to hear it."

"Well, my misfortune is none of your concern, I'm sure. I know you've been appointed Indian

Agent. Still hoping to end all this without bloodshed, are you?"

"Yes, General. I do, and I've brought some people that are going to help me do it."

"Good, good. I'm glad to hear it. I wish you all the luck in your new endeavor as Indian Agent." Matt could see the general was showing him the way out.

"Thank you for seeing me General, and I truly don't like to hear about you being relieved of your command."

"What really has me amazed about you Hutchins, is I hear you are a man with little education, raised by these savages and yet your reach is as far as the President in the White House. It's unbelievable. Officer of the day, please show

Mr. Hutchins out and see to it that his party is made comfortable. They'll be spending the night with us."

"Yes, Sir. Mr. Hutchins, if you'll follow me, sir?" As they walked, Matt could feel the animosity in the air. He was becoming annoyed with all the different looks he was getting from the soldiers.

"Captain?" Matt asked, "What's going on here? Have I done something or said something to offend all of you? All I'm trying to do is stop the bloodshed and hope I can talk peace with the Lakota. Is that doing wrong? To want to save lives instead of watching two nations tear one another apart?"

"No Mr. Hutchins," said the Captain. "I see nothing wrong with that, but the officers are worried about the outcome of the last engagement. With the General being relieved of this command, most of the officers are just out of West Point, and others are career, officers. This black eye on the Command doesn't look right in the records, and future appointments are based on records."

Captain Nelson overhearing some of the conversation, joins them. "Hello, Matt. Welcome back."

"Hello, Captain. I see you made it through it all, and you don't look worried."

"No. I'm not worried. These young officers just out of West Point were eager and bloodthirsty, so they took the field thinking it was going to be a cakewalk. They went by the book, but it didn't end well. The Lakota took off with a whole wagon load of rifles and ammunition, so they not only inflicted a lot of damage but now they're armed with the new repeating rifles. We've been praying we don't get hit again."

Chapter Twenty Three

Buffalo Robes gathered all the leaders of the Lakota together for a council. The scouting party reported seeing Matt enter the soldier camp with other white eyes.

Buffalo Robes began, "I have called you to altogether because my son has returned. He is in Soldiers camp as we speak and has sent the word he will be with us soon. When the sun begins to come out, we will look for him. As soon as he comes, the scouting party is to bring them here. He brings with him other white eyes, they are to go unharmed, but we must also be watchful. I have spoken."

Black Elk began, "My brothers. We have strong medicine now. We have killed many of the soldiers and counted many coups. The young warriors are eager to continue the fight. I say we should not wait."

Buffalo Robes speaks again, "Hear me. Our medicine is powerful, but we must listen to what Pahaska has to say. We sent for him to come, to get more time to pray to the spirits for snow. We must get that time."

Broken Nose had been silent and listened. Once a Great War Chief amongst the Lakota, he was now a sub-chief with one of the sub-bands that made up the Lakota speaks. "Hear me. I am old. I have lived for many flurries of snow, and I have seen many wars, many of the great ones that have fallen in battle, now hunt in the other place with the spirits. I walk the spirit trail and will join them soon. But I know this. When we do battle and lose a warrior, it takes many Snows to replace this one.

But the white eyes come more and more, they fill this place with many villages where there were once hunting ground for Tatanka. Now, as we travel here, I have seen many white eyes, but none of the Tatanka that makes the Lakota strong and fills our bellies. The Lakota should be in council with Pahaska. He is wise in the ways of both the Lakota and the whites. I have spoken."

There was much mumbling after hearing Broken Nose speak. Most were in agreement with him, but Black Elk needed to say more. "Yes, I honor Pahaska for his deeds as a warrior, and he is wise in the ways of the white eyes. I remember well the day Buffalo Robes found him. He was wrapped in a blanket with the paper of the Jesus spirit. Pahaska has great medicine with both the spirit worlds. I will hear him speak. I will look into the eyes of the ones who travel with him. I have spoken."

"Good," said Buffalo Robes, "The council agrees. We will spread the word among the people that Pahaska will be with us, and we will hold to our agreement to wait."

Many of the people were happy to hear this as word spread fast. Pahaska was good medicine for the Lakota. He was brave in battle and wise in council. Yet there were many sad hearts among the people who had lost their warrior in battle. Yet they had hope in their hearts for the talk of peace.

Many of the maidens and widows hoped Pahaska would invite them to sit under his blanket. Their discussion became excited. Storm Women heard about Matt's coming and was overjoyed. As

Buffalo Robes entered the teepee, she had many questions.

"How long will our son be with us?" she asked.

"We will sit in council and listen to his words. I cannot tell you how long. He brings with him others who are white eyes, so I know he brings the word for peace."

John D. Fie Jr

Chapter Twenty-Four

Matt, up before dawn was anxious to get started and began waking everyone. The sheriff and Charlie came out of their tent and headed for the cook fire with the coffee.

"Matt?" Charlie said a little gruffly, as they met him. "I'm gonna start calling him earlier." The sheriff laughed.

"Yep. Matt must have something against roosters letting him know it's time to get up. Maybe we should start calling him a rooster."

There was a loud roar from the mayor's tent.

Matt standing by the fire commented, "There he goes getting the day off to a rip-roaring start," Matt said laughing, "and here he comes."

"Mr. Hutchins," said the mayor. "Do you have something against waiting until the sun is up before waking everyone up?"

"Not at all, just thought you might enjoy a fresh cup of coffee before breakfast."

Then Charlie added, "Yeah, and you may want to be in the front of the line when they call breakfast. I think it's gonna be a long line."

"Alright. Alright. Enough with the jokes. I don't believe I'll be eating breakfast this morning with the ride we have before us. I've been thinking about my hair all night and how fond I am of it. We've already lost one from our party due to an upset stomach."

Matt and the Sheriff looked at one another, then Sheriff Fry says, "I'll handle this," and sets off to get the banker out of bed.

He enters the tent and jerks him out of bed. "I don't feel so good, leave me be." Came the bank managers response. He seemed very reluctant to go, and the sheriff thought there might be problems today. Something wasn't right because he was nervous, too nervous.

John D. Fie Jr

Chapter Twenty Five

Matt was keeping a close eye on the banker. He was acting very nervous, unlike the others who were just as unsure of this meeting.

Matt dropped back and began talking to him. "Something on your mind," he asked. "You're mighty jumpy about this meeting, have been from the start?"

Sheriff Fry, seeing Matt talking to the banker drops back and joins them.

"I'd be interested myself in knowing why you're so jumpy. Wouldn't be you got something to hide, now would it? You know I found something a while back. A conch. I see you're missing one." He dug into his pocket and pulls out the conch. "Looks like it matches the ones on your hat. Is this one yours?"

Matt watched his reaction, and a look of surprise was on the banker's face. "Sure looks similar to the one I'm missing. Where did you find it?" came his reply.

"Out in a canyon where Matt and I got dry-gulched by a couple of rustlers. Now, how do you suppose this conch got there?"

Matt started to ease Ole Friend onto his right side, watching him real close.

"Now don't do anything foolish," Matt told him. "Like trying to run 'cause you wouldn't get far anyway. Take a good look on the hill yonder. That scouting party has been with us and has been watching us since we left the Army camp. Why don't you hand over your six shooter and be real slow about doing it."

Suddenly Charlie shouted out. "Look, Matt, over yonder. We got company." Dancing Bear decided it was time to bring them to the camp.

Matt saw them approaching and told everyone, "Just sit easy and keep your hands away from your weapons.

"They're being cautious and coming slow, so don't do nothing stupid," Matt said.

"Sheriff, handcuff that fool or tie his hands. I don't want him to ruin this. I'm going out there to greet them." Moving off at a lope, Matt stops in front of the group and welcomes Dancing Bear.

"Ho ha he, Dancing Bear. It is a happy time to see you once again. All is well with the people?" he asked.

"Ho ha, he Pahaska. Yes, all is well. The people are eager to greet you. The old ones are happy of your coming, and the maidens are all hoping to share a blanket with you. The drums are beating, they hope for much dancing and joy."

"I bring with me friends the people can trust, and one I wish to find out about. To see if the people have seen him before. He is no friend."

"Yes, we will see Pahaska. He will stay with the dogs if he is not a friend. Come we go." The group joins Dancing Bear as he set a ground-eating lope with Charlie leading the pack horses and the sheriff leading the banker on his horse. Soon they were joined by another party. Matt could see their faces, all these young Warriors meant business. They had tasted battle and had bloodied scalps hanging from a few lances. He also spotted many of the new repeating rifles.

The mayor bouncing in the saddle didn't seem to have control of his horse. The horse on his own was keeping pace with the others.

Matt saw smoke signals, and he knew they were close to the camp. So it's true Matt thought, "Buffalo Robes has led the people into the mountain pass, and once the snow comes it will close, and there will be no way the Army can get to them. With plenty of good grass for the horses to graze and plenty of game to hunt, it will be an easy winter for them."

John D. Fie Jr

Chapter Twenty-Six

There was much excitement in the camp, Pahaska was back and the old ones rejoiced of the fun and good medicine that Pahaska brings to the people. However, there was some unease about the company he brought the people.

Once they were well into the camp, Matt saw Buffalo Robes, Black Elk and a few of the other sub-chiefs approaching. Turning to the others, Matt tells them, "Stay on your horses until I tell you different."

"Ho ha he! My Son," Buffalo Robes greets Matt with a hug. We heard of your return two periods of sleep ago. You first visit the soldier camp. Many eyes have been watching,"

Buffalo Robes steps back looking at him, "You bring with you white eyes, are they to be trusted? Do they speak with a straight tongue?"

"They are friends, my father," Matt explains. "They are the leaders of the white eye's village. But I bring one I am not sure of. I brought him for you to see. For the people to see. I also brought the sheriff. He enforces the white man's justice. If the one I'm not sure of has done bad with the Lakota, then the sheriff will enforce the white man laws on him."

Black Elk spoke up, "Ho ha he Pahaska. It is happy to see you once again. I will see this one you speak of. If it is true that he has done harm to the people, he is not welcome among us and will sleep with the dogs. Tomorrow when the sun rises we will let the women have their sport with him, then you may return him to make white man law on him. I have spoken."

Matt knew not to argue the matter and agreed, he pointed him out to the Chiefs. On Buffalo Robes orders, the banker was brought before them. The Warriors were dragging him, and he was pleading, asking Matt to help him. As he lay on the ground before the Chefs, Broken Nose spoke.

"Hear me. My eyes have seen this one. This one comes to make council with the soldier camp. He comes with two others, and they bring the white man Tatanka. But it is never enough to fill the bellies of the Lakota. These white eyes would come many times and drink the crazy water, like the soldiers. They force themselves on our women and tell the old ones they are stupid. They beat the people who speak back like dogs. For this one to sleep with the dogs is too good. I have spoken."

After hearing this, Matt asks his father. "Can the others get off their horses."

Buffalo Robes gives his approval, the warriors step forward and begin to greet the new arrivals.

The banker still laying on the ground begging Matt to help him. The Warriors on Black Elks orders took him away. As the others are led away, they could hear the screams of the bank manager.

The mayor was bewildered and asks Matt, "What will they do to him?"

"First they will strip him clean, tie his hands and then tie a rope around his neck and tie the other end to a tree. He'll be spending the night with the tribal dogs. The pecking order, as all dog packs, do when there is a new arrival is to show the new arrival whose, boss."

"Poor soul, isn't there anything we can do for him? I mean there must be something?" said the mayor sorrowfully.

"Not unless you want to join him. Tomorrow he'll be turned over to the women so they can have fun with him for a while. After the council, he'll be given over to the sheriff to take back and stand trial. Make yourselves comfortable, gentlemen. I've got to join Buffalo Robes and Storm Women. The women will bring you food, and you can walk around if you wish. Just remember to be respectful and try not to look at the maidens. They may take it the wrong way and if one of the women does seem to be showing you favor, don't insult her by refusing her gift. Don't walk around armed. Take off your gun belts."

Saying good night, Matt leaves them.

Chapter Twenty-Seven

The pipe was smoked first and then silence. Buffalo Robes began the council, by making his opening statement of the feelings of the people, then adding his own. "I have watched for many moons as the soldiers dishonor their words from the paper. They speak with a different tongue than what is on the paper. We have gone with empty bellies for too long. They take from us our young and tell them it is bad to speak the tongue of the Lakota. They say it is bad to follow the ways of the Lakota. These things we will not do. We will not talk of paper words. We will hear what my son has to say. I have spoken."

Matt began by greeting everyone and then begins. "I will not speak with paper words. I will talk to you about not fighting. I have sent my words to the Chief Soldier in Washington City, and he has held council with the Chief of all the white men. The Lakota know my words are true. The High Chief of the white man in the village of Washington has made me the Indian Agent. There will be no other to speak with the Lakota. The High Chief knows I am of the two villages and I understand the wants and needs of the Lakota. I have brought with me the leaders of the white man's village to the south. We have found a solution to no fighting. The soldiers are leaving and will not follow the Lakota. The Lakota will stay here to winter or as long as they like. This is not words of the paper, this is my words. I have spoken."

The Chiefs were overjoyed, and they talked among themselves. Buffalo Robes told Matt, "They should go and wait while the council speaks of these new words."

When the chiefs called them back, it was agreed with the council that Matt and Charlie would visit the village every month. If the Lakota needed to speak with Matt, they could send for him. Both sides were happy with this arrangement, and they would give it a trial period of six months. Then speak of paper words. Saying goodbye to the village, the peace party returned to town.

John D. Fie Jr

Chapter Twenty Eight

Matt and Charlie had made several trips to the village, and the town was now used to having neighbors to their north. The Army had made their retreat, and Matt was reporting directly to Washington. Washington had agreed to pay the local cattle ranchers every month to supply the Lakota with beef. The Lakota began trading with Charlie, and the store now had goods for sale made by the Lakota women.

Fry, joining Matt at the café, sits down at the table. "I got the banker safely to the Territorial prison. There wasn't a peep out of him the whole way there. I was hoping to get back in time for your big day. I didn't miss it, did I?"

Matt looked towards the kitchen and laughs, "No, she's excited as all get out. I don't think the days are passing fast enough for her. I've got another surprise for her after we're married. I got the word by telegraph today. Here she comes now, I'll tell you about it later."

Sally had seen the sheriff come in and gave him a little bit of time to have a few words with Matt.

As she approached the table, she said, "Hello Sheriff. Did you have a safe trip? I hope that scoundrel is locked away for a long time. Imagine him rustling, swindling and stealing from the very people he met and smiled at every day. I can't help but feel betrayed."

"You and a lot of others Sally," replied Fry. "But he's long gone and forgotten now. There is one good thing he did. He got the railroad headed this way. I'm pleased as a bowl of punch that he's gone and the two of you got together and decided to tie the knot. With Matt staying and helping out with the Lakota. I think we can look forward to Buffalo Flats growing and being a safe place to settle and live."

Made in the USA
Lexington, KY
09 August 2017